DANCING

WITH GHOSTS

Rita H Rowe

For John, who has been dancing with me for the last thirty years. Where you lead, I follow and where I lead you do the same. We will be dancing until the day we die, and well into the afterlife.

TABLE OF CONTENTS

PROLOGUE

The dance was complete.

The music was soft, so soft she could barely hear it anymore, echoing the rhythm of her heart. It was the last time she would have her hand in his, feel the firmness of his hold on the small of her back, as they spun in slow circles, lost in the dream. She knew she shouldn't, but she lay her head on his shoulder. He didn't move away and she let it linger, taking in the last breath of his skin, the touch of his starched collar, the soft blowing of his breath on her forehead. She drew back and looked up at his face, the slight smile on his lips now vanishing. In one swift movement, they were apart, facing each other.

It was done.

She curtsied, her head bent low, and when she looked up, he was gone.

CHAPTER 1

When driving on Thicket's Lane, Lovelet Manor seems miles away, but not a minute later, it rises behind the tall oak trees, announcing its presence in a most fantastical way.

That's exactly how Alex saw it, fantastic, like something out of an old book she'd read some years before, and she shrunk low in her minivan, wondering what she had gotten herself into. Stepping lightly on the brake, she looked around at the vast gardens, strewn with weeds and unkempt shrubs that were burnt by the sun, and her heart skipped a beat. There was going to be a lot of work for her to do, but this is what she was here for. A thrill of anticipation ran through her, replacing the stab of fear she'd tried to keep at bay. A new place, a whole new life.

She raised her foot off the accelerator and let the car slide down the stone driveway which was thick with dust, and it rolled to a stop just before the set of steps that led to a porch which encircled the house. She pulled up the park brake and craned her neck to locate the front door, of which she could only view the tip, which was an old-fashioned gilded pattern, set on a stone facade. A little shiver ran down her spine and she took a deep breath, relieved that no one was around.

She twisted the rear-view mirror to regard her reflection and smoothed down the red ringlet that kept falling over her eyes, and licking the tip of her index finger, wiped the smudges of mascara that stained the rim of her eye. 'Knew I shouldn't have put that god-awful stuff on,' she muttered to herself. She raised her eyebrows a couple of times to stretch out her face muscles and pinched her cheeks to give them colour. Her brown eyes stared back at her, her father's eyes, too large, taking over her small oval face. At least she also got his tanned skin, which concealed the blotches that appeared when she was nervous. And right now, she was nervous.

Taking a deep breath, she went for the door handle and started when she saw a tall, moustached man looming over the front of her car, his arms crossed, his eyebrows raised in bemusement, watching her. Alex bit her lip and opened the door, as the man moved to the side of the car to greet her.

Before Alex could say anything, he pointed to the edge of the driveway, where a path lay, almost hidden by an arch of more overgrown plants. 'Just drive through there. Milly will meet you out back.'

'Okay,' she mumbled, but he was already striding to the

front door, which she could now see was a giant wooded panel which looked like it would take a crane to move.

That must be the man whom she had spoken to on the phone, the one who interviewed her. Samuel, he had said his name was; oddly cold, even on the phone. She swallowed and drove to where he had gestured, just squeezing her car through the little gap between the arch. Another winding road, more like a curved track, unpaved, ran parallel to the house, and she followed it, wondering where it was taking her and how long it would be until she got there. She figured it would take a long time to circle this mansion.

She questioned again whether she had done the right thing coming here. She didn't know these people, they could be psychopathic murderers for all she knew, but what she did know was she had to leave Melbourne, get as far away as possible from there and everything it held for her. She blinked hard to keep from the thoughts that tried to penetrate her brain from the moment she had left, more than four hours earlier.

As she slowly turned a sharp corner, she was upon another wooden set of doors, much smaller, one of which was slightly ajar. No one was around and Alex wondered if Milly, whoever she was, was informed of her arrival. She stopped the car and looked at her phone, wondering if she should call Samuel, but by his sound of his abrupt instruction, she thought better of it. Her finger automatically scrolled to Nicholas's number and hovered there for a moment. It was the only one she'd put into her new phone, strange as he was the only one she was trying to leave.

'Hello.' She heard a voice call and looking up, Alex saw a woman, a dishcloth in hand, waving to her.

Alex dropped her phone in her bag and waved back, breathing a sigh of relief, and got out of the car. 'Hi, I'm Alex,' she called and hurried to the woman she assumed was Milly. She put out her hand, and the portly woman laughed at the offering, shaking out her own, little fluffs of flour dropping from them.

'Sorry, hands are a mess.' She waved them about again. 'I'm Milly. Come on in.'

Alex felt a surge of relief. Milly, who seemed to be about the age her mother would have been, was smiling in welcome, far removed from the stilted Samuel. 'What about my things?' Alex looked back at her car, which held all her worldly goods.

'Leave it. Rory will help you in a bit. He's just gone to the horses.' She motioned to her right and Alex looked over a spread of grass, where a large shed, which looked like a dollhouse, stood in the distance.

'You have horses?' Alex's eyes widened.

'Uh-huh,' Milly replied and shook her head in the direction of the house. 'They love those things, especially Rory.

He's even trying to teach the young one. Too little for riding if you ask me, but no one asks me,' she muttered and motioned for Alex to follow. 'Come on, I'll show you around. Let me just wash this off my hands.'

Alex looked back to her car, where she had left everything, including her phone and purse, and Milly, noticing her hesitation, chuckled.

'Your things are fine. No thieves here,' she said and Alex blushed.

She followed Milly into a dark alcove that gave her the shivers and out into a large kitchen. Alex's eyes widened. She had never seen such a big room, save for the dance hall, that she hadn't been to in over fifteen years. The cream-coloured walls resembled fresh butter, perhaps helped by the buttery aroma that floated about. She inhaled deeply, savouring the fusion of smells, and spotting two loaves of freshly baked bread, felt her stomach rumble and her mouth water. The sheen of stainless steel dazzled her, the spotless sink, and multiple benches, one of which was strewn with flour and eggs.

'Baking day,' explained Milly, sounding apologetic, as she saw Alex eye the only area of the kitchen that wasn't polished to perfection.

'Smells good,' she said, wondering who Milly actually was in this house. The maid? The cook? But she already liked the rosy-cheeked woman with silver hairs popping out of her hairnet, her ample bottom hopping from side to side as she took little steps on tiny feet. She reminded her of Mrs Potts from *Beauty and the Beast*, and a faraway thought invaded her mind.

'I'm the housekeeper, slash cook,' said Milly and Alex wondered if she was a mind reader too. 'Come on. Mr Samuel will be waiting in the hall.'

'You call him Mr?' asked Alex and immediately wished she hadn't. It sounded impertinent and she was the newcomer, the paid outsider. This woman looked like she had resided here for a long time.

'Always have,' said Milly and shrugged.

'Am I supposed to call him that too?'

Milly shrugged again and led Alex through a dimly lit hallway which didn't seem to have much purpose and was treated as such, its light-grey walls not adorned with a single ornament, a solitary light bulb at the entrance leading them forward. They walked through a series of doors until they were abruptly in a large hallway, facing Samuel, his back straight, his lips pursed in what looked like irritation. He was a good-looking man, had light-brown eyes that could have been quite pleasant, but which bore an air of arrogance. He held his hands behind his back and Alex wondered if they had interrupted his pacing. He nodded quickly to acknowledge them and Alex put out her hand again, but he had already turned away, striding to a door which Alex realised was the front door, and she wondered if it would have been easier to just come in through it in the first place. Still, she followed him out to the wide porch and turned around to Milly, who had disappeared.

'Hello, Alexandra ...?'

'Alex is fine,' she interrupted, and a little smirk crossed his lips.

'I'm Samuel.' She wondered why he had waited until now to introduce himself properly, why he hadn't done so on meeting her in the driveway.

'So, I call you Sam?' she said, trying to break the tension with a light-hearted quip.

He didn't seem to find it amusing. 'Samuel is fine.' He rested his hands on the stone balustrade and faced the garden, frowning.

Alex cleared her throat in embarrassment—at least she didn't have to call him Mr. She looked up and her breath caught. Beyond the stone steps, of which there must have been at least ten, a fountain stood, and beyond that, a hedge almost as tall as the second storey of the house, a maze zigzagging through the expanse of the garden, of which she could see no end.

'Where do the grounds end?' she asked, now worried

about what she really had gotten herself into.

He ignored her question. 'Rory was going to take you around to show you the place, but he's still not back.' Alex could hear the impatience in his voice and hoped Rory, whoever he was, would hurry back. She thought about the belongings still in her car. It would be getting dark soon and she was hoping to have some time to unpack. She still had no idea where she would be sleeping; there had been no conversation about that over the phone, except that she would be living on the grounds. For all she knew, she could be living in a shack in the middle of nowhere, perhaps over on the other end of the garden. She hoped it had a bathroom, she needed one now.

'Um, what should I do?' she ventured, trying to fill the silence that was deafening above the swishing of the trees that surrounded the house. She stood behind him, not quite sure of what to say next; she seemed to be saying everything wrong anyway.

He sighed in exaggeration, and Alex could feel her own annoyance growing. 'I can show you some of it.' He looked skyward. 'It's going to be getting dark soon.'

Alex followed his gaze and noticed that the clouds had come in. She looked at her watch; it was only four thirty in the evening—it would still be bright in Melbourne. A breeze wafted past, and she felt a shiver, looking down at her yellow blouse and jeans. She suddenly wanted to go to the bathroom really badly, realising she hadn't stopped to relieve herself all the way here. But she followed him as he walked down the eleven steps—she counted them—until they hit the driveway and she glanced up to view the sculpture, a replica of Michelangelo's *David*. It was tall and she stretched her neck backwards to see to the top of it. When she turned back, Samuel was already a few metres in front of her and she hurried to catch up to him. He was an intimidating figure, his back still rod straight, his black hair short and almost stuck to his scalp, his hands braced behind him. And the way he walked, like he was commanding an army. She felt a shiver again; this time she wasn't sure it was just the cold and rubbed at her arms.

They were at the edge of the driveway, heading through another hedged archway and Samuel had to dip slightly to fit under it. In a moment they had come out the other side and Alex halted and sucked in her breath.

'Wow,' she said, gazing at the expanse of land covered in circles of garden beds.

'It's big, yes,' said Samuel and pointed at one they had neared. 'These will need to be done, as will the rest. I don't expect you to do the lawns, but I will expect you to trim the trees. We have the equipment.' He pointed to the right of the house. 'A shed near the horses, behind there,' he said and Alex figured it must be the one Milly had pointed to before.

'No problem,' replied Alex, a little worried about how she was supposed to cope with so much, but the sight of the garden gave her a thrill, even though roses hung on to their stems limply and what should have been green was anything but. She could bring these back to life, she could nurture, love, and help them grow. It was a lot, but no time limit had been mentioned, so she assumed this was an ongoing position. Well, this place certainly needed some love.

'I will need it to be presentable by December.'

'Okay?' She wondered what was happening in December, but he didn't seem to expect a question and he didn't elaborate further. It wasn't her business, but did it mean that she would be out of a job come then? She wished she had discussed the fine print over the phone, but it was too late; besides, she knew she had taken this job without thinking it through. There had been no time for that. She would work something out when she knew more.

They walked around through a series of curves and straights, and Alex could feel a sense of excitement mounting. Samuel pointed to areas, all areas really, and told her they would need doing. But Alex was lost in her own world, squealing at the camellia beds, rubbing her hands at the bottlebrushes and smiling at the benches with names on their backrests.

'How gorgeous,' she cried and dropped to her knees to

17

sniff a spread of lavender. She looked up at Samuel, who was looking down at her with what she could only discern as condescension. She cleared her throat and stood up, dusting the mud from her knees, and a shiver hit the back of her neck, travelling down to her thighs. She looked up and before her, a few metres in the distance, stood a gazebo, a grand edifice commanding attention, and she gave in to its command, her mouth dropping slightly, her head dizzy. She took a step towards it but the voice of Samuel, hurrying her on, snapped her out of her trance.

She followed him the rest of the way in silence as he led her through a series of twists and turns, her excitement rising, yet the amount of work to be done scaring her, and suddenly they were back at the edge of the driveway. She looked up, and the enormity of the mansion, silhouetted by the setting sun, left her jaw slack. She'd been surrounded by large houses and mansions during her childhood, but she'd not seen anything like this. The sheer size of the house was imposing, manor was the right word for it, she nodded to herself, and she let her eyes wander over the hulking structure. The stone house curved halfway around the driveway, a balustrade surrounding the entire front porch, and on the left side, four garage doors. She raised her head to view the top as she counted the storeys—five—which came together in the shape of a steeple with a few windows that were lit dotting its façade. One of them was ajar, a sliver of laced curtain hovering in and out of it breezily, and she felt a slight chill again.

'Who else lives here?' she asked despite herself.

'Now it's just my brother and his wife and kids, two of them.' He said it without warmth and Alex knew there had to be a story there, but she was certainly not going to ask this man who had so very coldly shown her around the grounds without a thought to ask her about herself, but it suited her just fine. She wasn't about to reveal anything to someone she'd just met. In fact, it was better there was no connection between her new life and the one she'd left behind. 'Here he is now,' said Samuel, lifting his chin, his lips pursing.

Alex turned around to see a tall, rugged man approach in riding breeches, his black hair wavy, his stride large. He looked very much like Samuel, except he had a smile on his lips that added a charm to an otherwise ordinary face, and he waved as he approached them.

'You must be Alexandra,' he said and took her hand, shaking it heartily.

'Alex,' she said and smiled, a flood of relief rushing through her at his demeanour.

'Rory,' he said. 'Have you met Cheryl and the girls?'

'No,' Samuel answered for her. 'She just got here.' His tone was clipped and if anything, he was even more detached, if that were possible, with his brother than he was with her.

Alex didn't want to correct him. They had been walking around for at least an hour, and she was freezing, dusk setting upon them without warning. She wished she had ducked into the bathroom before they left the house, but she didn't know where that was. No one had shown her and anyway, Samuel seemed to be in such a hurry and in such a foul mood, she didn't want to annoy him further. She'd even sneaked a longing look at an overgrown shrub and wondered whether he would notice if she disappeared for a few seconds to relieve herself. Of course she wouldn't have, but she was past desperation, even at that point.

Rory took off his coat and placed it on Alex's shoulders. 'You look like an icicle,' he said and rubbed his hands together. 'Quite different in Melbourne, isn't it?'

'I'm okay,' said Alex. She didn't want to feel like a damsel in distress—damsel, such a lost word, but quite at home in this atmosphere, this house, these gardens, this mood, complete with a pair of duelling rivals. She nevertheless accepted the offering without argument.

'I got stuck at the creek. It's quite beautiful this time of year. Maybe we can all go one day before winter sets in,' said Rory, seemingly oblivious to Samuel's mood, and walked with them back to the house.

'I have to go,' said Samuel, as they got to the door. 'Goodbye.' And he disappeared.

'He doesn't live here,' Rory explained, and Alex felt a sense of relief. 'Sorry you had to deal with him,' he said, an apologetic smile resting on his lips. 'Come on, let's meet the others. Hey, are you hungry?'

'I am a little,' said Alex, 'but I really need to use the bathroom.'

CHAPTER 2

'Garver comes every two weeks to go over the lawns,' Rory told her as they walked into the house after bidding goodbye to the grumpy Samuel. 'So you don't have to do that, obviously, even though the ride-on mower can be fun. You should try it one day, not so hard to manoeuvre. But you get to ride the golf cart whenever you want. You will need that to get around.' He looked at Alex's scrunched-up face and laughed. 'Right down the hallway,' he said, pointing to a door, and Alex assumed he was pointing to the toilet. She almost ran.

As she washed her hands, she glimpsed herself in the mirror and her eyes widened in shock. She had been wandering around with her new employer all that time with a streak of mascara that she clearly hadn't succeeded in clearing off her face. And her hair! She looked like a mad witch, red curls defying gravity, frizz already taking hold in the damp of the evening. She tried to smooth the waves, but they kept bouncing back, and she twisted and tucked the locks as much as she could behind her ears.

'Cheryl!' She could hear Rory calling his wife and Alex steeled herself for more drama. It was an odd assortment of people she had met in the last couple of hours: a harried maid, who gave away nothing; a nasty, monosyllabic man who clearly would have rather been doing anything else than showing her around; and the brother, a jovial, welcoming fellow. She hoped Cheryl would be like her husband. She couldn't guess at the exact age of Rory, but she figured he was around thirty, not much older than her, so his wife would probably be around the same.

'Daddy!' A little girl, dressed in red striped pyjamas, came bounding past as Alex stepped back into the foyer, and leapt into Rory's arms.

'Cathy girl. What have you been up to? Where's your mother?' he said after he twirled her around, kissed her cheek and placed her on the floor. He smiled with warmth when he saw Alex come in. 'Cathy, this is Alexandra, Alex. She's going to be our new gardener; well, I think there's another proper word for it. Horticulturalist?'

'Gardener is fine,' said Alex, holding her hand out to the girl who looked no older than six. She was a little perturbed at the way this family interacted with her, the help, and wasn't quite sure of how to reciprocate. Should she remain silent? Should she mimic their efforts? She thought she'd already be settling into her new abode, wherever that was, away from the residents of this place.

'Nice to meet you,' said Cathy, who smiled sweetly, her long dark hair flouncing around her as she gave a little curtsy. Alex forgot her qualms and bounced down to her haunches, completely taken with the little thing.

'Where were you?' came a tired voice behind Alex and she turned around to see a woman with the blackest, most shiny hair she had ever seen. The pale face, absurd in its frame, did a double take as she noticed Alex and she smiled a little smile, her grey eyes lighting up. 'Oh, hi, you must be Alex. Milly told me you came today.'

'Hello,' said Alex and held out her hand, but Cheryl had already turned back to her husband. 'Netty's not doing well today. The pain was worse than ever. I wish you would have come back sooner.'

'Sorry, darling,' said Rory and lifted Cathy up again. 'I'll see to her now.' He looked at Alex. 'Have you had dinner? We eat quite early here, but if you're hungry, Milly can rustle something up for you. She's still here.'

Alex was hungry; now she felt it more acutely than before, the urge of having to go to the toilet taking her mind off her rumbling tummy. She nodded and looked around, not remembering how to get back to the kitchen. Cheryl noticed her confusion and pointed down one of the hallways and Alex nodded and travelled back through the path from which she had come, which was even more creepy now that she was on her own.

She found the kitchen smelling like a bakery now, and a range of cookies was arranged on one of the benches, fly cloth spread over them. Milly was taking off her apron and looked up as Alex walked in.

'Hungry?' she asked.

'Yeah, a little. But my stuff from my car. I have to get it out first.'

'All done. Rory put it all in your room,' said Milly and Alex wondered again where exactly that was. 'He came back a little after you left.' She took out a leg of roast chicken from the fridge and put it in the microwave. Then she arranged a salad, gesturing for Alex to sit on a stool, which she did with relief. 'Oh, they have you staying in the main house. Mr Samuel is cleaning up the servants' quarters …' She rolled her eyes. 'Well, I don't think there were any servants' quarters, just a three-bedroom, which was used for the help in the mid-fifties. Then it became a guest house, then it just became run-down. There were even squatters in there a few times …'

Alex almost swallowed the food without chewing, she was ravenous, and she listened with interest as Milly nattered on while she circled her dishcloth on the sparkling bench.

'Aaron, that's my man, comes sometimes to the manor, you might see him,' she said. 'Just a warning because he has the tendency to scare people off. He's a big lout.' She smiled with tenderness. 'Crazy long moustache that he won't get rid of. He comes to look at the horses and take care of Scamper. Have you met Scamper yet?'

Alex shook her head, taking a swig of apple juice that tasted so fresh, she wondered if she had missed the apple trees in the garden.

'Then there's Joel and Freddy. They're my sons ...' She narrowed her eyes at Alex. 'How old are you, love?'

'Twenty-nine,' said Alex, bemused by the matchmaking look on the woman.

'Ah,' Milly replied, nodding, and Alex could almost hear her doing the maths in her head. 'Well, anyway, they are loafers. Not ready to take a wife, either of them. But they are kind boys and I couldn't keep them in the country forever. We live just past Chernut and they wanted to experience city life for a while.' She shook her head in perplexity. She narrowed her eyes at Alex again. 'Why did you leave Melbourne?'

Alex choked on the lettuce she'd just deposited in her mouth. 'Um ...'

'It's okay, eat up,' said Milly, seeming to understand

Alex's hesitance. 'Anyway, I don't understand what those boys want in that place, so big, so noisy, Melbourne. I couldn't imagine going back there.' She sighed and lifted her shoulders. 'But come December, who knows?'

'What's in December?' asked Alex.

'Who knows,' Milly repeated and took Alex's plate, which looked near clean. 'Are you still hungry, love?'

Alex shook her head. 'No, no! That was too much and delicious.' She drew breath in satisfaction. 'Thank you. Just what I needed.'

'You look tired,' said Milly. 'Come on. I'll take you to your room.' She led Alex out of the kitchen and after showing her the bathroom and leading her to her room, Milly left with a 'goodnight and sweet dreams'.

****

The room was big, so big that if she arranged everything she had from her old flat in here, it would still look empty. She hung her few clothes in the spacious closet and spread them out to make her feel like she actually owned clothes. Three sets of overalls, two pairs of jeans, six tops in assorted colours and beneath them, two pairs of gardening boots, a pair of heels—why she brought them, she didn't understand—and two pairs of flats, one black, one white. It was a modest wardrobe, but what did she need more clothes for? She didn't know anyone in this place, and she had never really been the socialising type anyway.

Opening her suitcase of frames and ornaments, things that were supposed to make her feel some comfort, she saw the face of Nicholas looking up at her, his mouth wide, his blue eyes creased as the sun hit them, smiling for the camera. She felt a movement in her heart and turned the frame over quickly. She rummaged around and after finding the pile of letters held together by a rubber band, she quickly zipped the bag, leaving the rest of it as it was, and tucked it under the bed. She could leave the rest of the unpacking for another day. Everything was still too fresh.

After tucking the letters into her bedside table, she hopped into bed, pulling the covers over her and holding them tight against her chin, her eyes on the door. She was so cold, she didn't want to get out of bed again, but she breathed a sigh of frustration and dashed to it, trying to twist the key in the door that was already turned. She had to make sure. It was her first night in a strange house with even stranger people. Besides, it was habit. She felt her bladder pinch and wished that there was an ensuite, but why would there be in a house like this, not a single modern restoration to be seen, not even central heating.

The bathroom was only a few steps away from her room, but she wished she didn't have to wander around a strange house and bump into people she barely knew, even though she was assured there was no one else on the third floor. Rory and his wife and children occupied the first and Milly went home to her family at the end of the day, after making sure everyone was fed and the cleaning was done.

Alex rushed back to the king-sized bed and closed her eyes, going through the motions of the day that had just passed and wondering what she was in for in this house with its array of people, some of whom she hadn't met yet. A warm, sweet maid, a happy man with a sickly-looking wife, a well child and a not-so-well child, from what she'd gathered in that short conversation, and a cold brother, who didn't even live in this massive house. She did wonder about its size, so large with rooms she probably would never see, with such a little family living in it. She curled into the mattress, so soft it almost wrapped around her, now warm, the soft sheets and heavy blankets giving her a feeling of comfort, of safety, and she smiled to herself. Unbidden, the image of Nicholas swam before her and her chest gave an involuntary thud. Just a week ago, he was beside her in her bed, his breath on her neck, his soft snore drowning out the memories that used to haunt her. A tear escaped and slid onto her pillow and she swiped at her cheek angrily.

She turned her thoughts from him. She was an expert in

doing that now. She had to focus on what was going to happen, not what may have been. She wondered about December; she'd need to find that out as soon as possible. Would that mean her time here was done? That was eight months away, she had time, but she would still have to plan what to do next. Maybe move further up, perhaps leave the state, go to Queensland. But she didn't like the weather there, too balmy; she remembered it when she was there as a teenager on holidays with her parents … She couldn't return to Melbourne, too much had happened and if she saw Nicholas again, she may be tempted to run into his arms, to forget her idea of a new life.

A clicking noise pricked up her ears and Alex shivered despite the cosy cocoon of her bed. She tiptoed to the door from where the sound came and held her ear against it, but nothing more came so she circled to the window and, brushing back the lace curtain, looked into the night. Her chest made a little bump when she caught sight of the gazebo, silhouetted in the moonlight, and she could feel goosebumps forming on her arms. A loud thump from somewhere in the house jolted her out of the trance she had found herself in, and she released the curtains, falling into the armchair beside the window. She breathed deeply, trying to compose herself, trying to convince herself that it was just the jitters of being in a foreign place. She wished the servants' quarters were still used for their original purpose. She would have felt much more at home in a little place by herself, than surrounded by a bunch of empty rooms in a massive old house.

She opened the bedside drawer and took out the pile of letters, reading the last one as she always did before she wrote again. She didn't like to repeat news and this one was written three days ago.

April 13

Dear Mum and Pa,

I think I'm ready to go. I've packed and I just have to load the car. It's been awful though. He is everywhere. I've packed a box of his stuff and I wanted to give up my idea altogether. Then I almost kept his sweater, the green one with that awful pattern, but I didn't. I packed it with his things. I'll send it on the day I leave. I wish you could tell me if I'm doing the right thing. I don't know anymore. There are so many doubts, but I've trusted myself before, and I have to again; there's no one else I can trust.

I almost called him today, but what could I say? Sorry? Goodbye? And I was more worried about what he would say back. See ya? Don't call me again? Maybe he wouldn't have answered his phone, ignored me? I have to remain strong though, and it's working, not thinking about him. I can focus on what I need to do. But I know I hurt him so much. And then he hasn't called me in a week. So what does that mean? That I'm right? I was right all along? That I never should have come so close to giving him everything? He loved me, I know he did, but I can't risk that anymore.

I hope I have your blessing, that you are still rooting for me, that you're on my side. I will get over this too.

Won't write for a couple of days …

She couldn't continue, her eyes blurred with tears, her heart breaking all over again. She tucked the letter away and picked up her notepad, beginning on a blank page.

April 18

Dear Mum and Pa,

Too early for anything new to say. Just about to spend my first night in this place. Strange people, strange house, but I think I'm going to be okay. Gotta go, must try to sleep. Big day ahead tomorrow.

Love you, Blanche.

She crossed out Blanche.

Alexandra.

She folded the note and placed it atop the pile in her bedside drawer. She smiled at the name and let her tongue circle around her new name.

Alexandra. It was a name she had always wanted as a child after she read it in a book, but her parents had preferred Blanche, an old-fashioned name, a moniker passed down from her grandmother, whom she had never met. Now she had the chance to actually use the name she'd always wanted. She just hoped she would remember when she was introduced to anyone new. She had rehearsed it many times back in her flat in Melbourne, repeated it over and over in front of the mirror.

She said it now and closed her eyes. Sleep came easy to her tonight.

CHAPTER 3

The alarm on her phone buzzed and Alex jumped in fright even though it was familiar to her, but for a moment she was lying next to Nicholas, his warm body spooning hers, his breath waving strands of her hair that tickled her neck. Her heart dropped when she realised she wasn't where she was a week ago and Nicholas was hundreds of miles away. A touch of regret made her curl into her body but before it could take over, she threw off the blankets and leapt out of bed.

'Stop it!' she scolded herself while she made her bed. She wandered to the window, where dawn was trying to break through the heavy trees that lay across the horizon. She stretched and turned to begin getting ready for the day, but something caught her eye and she looked back through the window. Opening the curtain, her eyes scanned the garden, stopping at the gazebo which now glowed a shade of violet, and Alex felt a little shiver. It beckoned to her; she felt a longing to go to it and made a mental note to check it out. She took a deep breath and set out for her first day of work.

'So, Milly ...'

'Yes, love?' said Milly, her head still in the fridge.

'How old is this house?'

'It was built more than a hundred years ago.' Milly put the butter on the tray in three little blobs, next to fried eggs and bacon. 'Are you sure you want to eat in here?' She looked down at Alex with a frown.

'Yes, I prefer to.' Alex didn't want to impinge on the time of the family who would probably feel awkward with a strange face suddenly at their table, and she wasn't sure if it was the done thing, the residents of the house dining with the help. She looked at the spread of food. 'Do they eat that every day?'

Milly snorted and put her hand to her chest. 'No, of course not. They would have heart attacks if that were the case. No, today's special. Cathy is beginning grade one. She should have started in February but she had some catching up to do. Rory asked her what she wanted to begin her first day of primary school and she said bacon and eggs. So bacon and eggs it is.' She shrugged. 'I'll be back,' she said, picking up the tray, and Alex moved to open the door for her, but Milly shook her head. 'No, no, I've been doing this forever,' she said and bumped open the door with her generous hip.

Alex smiled and picked up her bacon, something she rarely had, and nodded. It was delicious. She looked about her and wondered whether she had time for a run; she didn't want to lose her fitness. Running was the only thing that kept her back from crying in pain from the continual bending over that gardening required and it was the only form of exercise she ever did. Besides, she enjoyed it; it freed her mind, the breeze blowing past her ears, the air in her face, heading towards something and towards nothing. The thoughts that tried to pierce her brain were kept at bay when she ran, just like when she danced. But she couldn't do that anymore, so running it was.

Milly pushed her way back into the kitchen with a frown.

'What is it, Milly?'

'No, nothing.' The old woman plastered a smile on her face and Alex wondered what had happened.

'So, Milly ...' began Alex.

'What is it, love?' Milly put the tray into the large sink that looked like a wash basin in a laundry.

'About the house,' said Alex, wondering if it were too soon to question anything. She had only been here one night. 'I just ... I think I heard things ...' Alex felt stupid. She couldn't even think of how to describe what she'd heard, and more, what she'd felt.

Milly turned around, a curious expression on her face. 'Like what?'

'I don't know really …' She tugged at a loose string on the end of her folded sleeve. 'Like a knocking, like maybe a window that wasn't locked … or something.'

'It's an old house. Things rattle and creak. Rory and Cheryl have lived here for a while.' Milly rested her wet hand on her hip and Alex could see her thinking. 'Rory all his life, but Cheryl … let's see now … they have been married, I think, about fifteen years, something like that. But they won't think of getting anything new. They want to keep its "charm". Samuel, on the other hand …' She shook her head and put her hands back in the soapy water.

Alex thought about her room which was icy last night. 'Oh, okay. I thought maybe something was open somewhere.'

'Could have been Netty.'

'Oh, the other daughter. I haven't met her yet.' She saw Milly's shoulders go up in another shrug. No answer was forthcoming. Alex took her plate and glass to the sink and Milly took it from her.

'Leave it there, love, I'll wash it with the others.'

'Are you sure?' Alex wasn't used to people doing things for her, except for … No, she couldn't think about him.

'Alex!' Cathy's voice resounded from the door and Alex turned to see the little girl rush to her.

Alex smiled, surprised the little girl, whom she had known for all of a day, was so excited to see her. 'First day of school?' She bent down to eye level with Cathy, whose hair today was in tight ringlets. 'Your hair looks beautiful.'

'So does yours!'

Alex gave her a wry smile and pulled at one of her unruly curls, which she'd tried to pin back with a clip this morning but which had already fallen onto her forehead.

'Morning, Cathy,' said Milly sternly.

'Good morning, Milly,' said Cathy in a formal tone and turned back to Alex. 'Hey, I don't have to go for another hour or something, Mum says. Have you seen the house yet?'

'I haven't, but I will take a tour later,' she replied, wondering if the girl knew the definition of tour.

'Can I take you for a tour now?'

'But aren't you meant to be getting ready for school?'

'I think I got up too early. Come,' she said, grabbing Alex's hand, and Alex turned to Milly, who was trying to stifle a laugh.

'Sure, a quick one, because I have to get to work.'

She followed Cathy through the cold, dim hallway and out into the foyer, which looked so very different from yesterday, a bright light shining through the large windows from which the thick green curtains were drawn.

'This is the front,' said Cathy, waving her arm about without stopping. 'And this is the living room,' she said, leading Alex to a massive space, and Alex looked upward, marvelling at the high ceiling, patterns of angels adorned on the cornices. The smell of freshly cut roses wafted through the room and Alex glanced at the window, which was open, through which the smell floated, to see yellow roses, fresh and hearty, peeking through the glass. *Well, those are certainly being looked after,* she thought, and wondered by whom.

'That's Daddy's chair.' Cathy pointed to a well-worn armchair that faced the front of the house. Alex looked around at the comfortable-looking sofa, a light shade of yellow, and noticed a wall unit, a number of pictures placed on them. She was curious and wanted to see them, but there would be time for that later.

Cathy pulled on Alex's arm and Alex followed again, curious and enchanted with this old-fashioned home, but her mind now on the work she needed to get to. Samuel clearly thought he had given her enough information before he left and she felt a cringe at the thought of the cold man, as well as another sense of relief that he didn't live here. She pushed him from her mind, hoping he didn't visit often. Today she was excited about going through the garden in the clear light of day, at her own pace, without the grouchy Samuel rushing her on.

'That's the dining room,' said Cathy with another wave of her arm. 'We don't really eat there. It's just for company.'

Alex smiled. She knew the little girl was just imitating what her mother would have said. She looked at the twelve-seater oak table, its chairs a green velvet, wondering if it ever got filled, and her attention was caught by a framed photograph on a table beside the French doors. This one she couldn't help but go to.

'Who is this?' she asked, looking into the face of a thirty-something-year-old man, standing against a gazebo, no, *the* gazebo, the same one she had seen last night and this morning, daring her to approach it. The black-and-white photograph showed the man wore a broad cravat, set against the white of his shirt, a tux jacket hung loosely over his arm. He was handsome, looked stern, yet a smile played on his lips, and Alex peered at it more closely, drawn to the smile, and she felt her heart pull.

'That's my grandpa,' Cathy said and tugged Alex's arm impatiently. She let herself be led away reluctantly into another room, a large hall, and Alex froze, gaping at the wooden floors, polished, shiny. 'This is the dance hall.'

Alex's legs quivered, and her breath came in short spurts; she leaned against the doorway, her ears buzzing. Another part of her life that she didn't want to remember, memories hitting her at the most unexpected times.

'Alex, come,' said Cathy, trying to pull her in, but Alex held tight to the doorframe.

'Can we do the rest later?' she asked shakily and backed out of the room.

'Just one more,' Cathy replied and skipped out of the room, taking Alex down a hallway to a large set of doors, which were closed.

'Cathy, where are you?' Alex heard the voice of Cheryl, which sounded like it was coming from very far away.

'Oh, I have to go now. Later can I show you again?' She looked up eagerly at Alex and she nodded, trying to smile.

Cheryl came into view, her hair pinned back tightly, a sharp black suit fitting snugly on her tiny frame, a little black pair of heels clicking on the floorboards. 'There you are,' she said to Cathy and turned to Alex. 'Sorry, um …' She suddenly seemed to be stuck for words. 'I should have shown you around, shouldn't I?'

'No, it's fine.' Alex was glad for the distraction, her heartbeat beginning to return to its normal rhythm. 'Cathy wanted to. Sorry I kept her.'

'No, no, don't be sorry.' Cheryl seemed to be more apologetic than she should have been, twiddling the tips of her fingers together. 'She kept you from your own work.'

'Oh, well, I got up too early,' Alex said. 'And I think the whole house did. Cathy's first day at school. How exciting.'

'Yes …' Cheryl looked distracted again and looked around for Cathy, who had already skipped away. 'Well, good luck,' she said and hurried out.

Alex suddenly wondered if she could find her way back to the kitchen but was relieved when she found the entrance to the hallway after a few twists and turns through the house, and by the time she reached the kitchen, her nerves had calmed down.

After Milly poured hot coffee into her flask, Alex set off to explore her new life.

CHAPTER 4

The shed, which looked like a little shack in the distance, was anything but. Alex opened the door, which welcomed her with a creak of relief, and she grinned. It probably wasn't used very much, if the state of the gardens was anything to go by. Her eyes widened, not just at the size of the shed, but at the state of it. Boxes of what, she didn't know, were packed on top of each other, crumbling from moisture and their weight. A large blue tin box sat in the middle of the shed and Alex peered into it and screwed up her face. These were the implements she had to work with. Well, she would have to spend some time sorting them out—not today. She turned her head and saw bags of newly acquired mulch and potting mix leaning against the side of the shed. Loads of it! Clearly they had no idea what to get, but to his credit, Samuel had listened when she asked for it. Just not so much!

Pushing away cobwebs that seemed to be attracted to her hair, she came upon a tractor, which seemed to be leaning to one side. Beyond that was the promised golf cart, a tray secured behind the driver's seat, and Alex inspected it, turning on the ignition and placing herself on the padded seat. She grinned again. This was going to be fun; she just hoped she could manoeuvre it properly, she'd never driven one herself, had just been a passenger when Nicholas had taken her to the club on a couple of occasions. She stroked the steering wheel and let herself indulge in the thought of him for a moment, wondering where he was and more importantly, how he was. Was he worried? Maybe she should have explained in person ... Then she shook her head free. It was done. She got out of the cart and went in search of the tools she would need today, probably not much, considering she was just going out to inspect the damage.

She shielded her eyes from the sun as she drove out, irritated that she didn't think to bring her straw hat out from her room, but she had been in a hurry to get started today. The sun was dazzling now and the empty fields on the other side of the garden reflected its glory. She was tempted to drive a little further up to the stables and run her hand over the nose of the horse that poked out of its lodging, but there would be time for that later. *There would be a lot to explore*, she thought, as she looked over at the never-ending spread of grass disappearing over the horizon.

A new hope hit her heart and she smiled at the feeling; it had been a long time since she had felt like this. She moved slowly around the grounds, taking note of the things that needed to be tended to immediately, which was pretty much all of it, from the garden beds, which were hard and dry, to the planter boxes that sat along the stone walls, in which lay dried-up plants, barely recognisable. She wondered who had tended to all this before. She marked each area on her pad; she would need a system, not go into it willy-nilly, even though she was tempted to stop at every turn. She wondered why the family hadn't just employed a team, but on an ongoing basis; this would probably have been best. She was excited, up for the challenge, and couldn't wait to get started. She would first have to work her way through this maze, but carefully wound her way around the stone path in the little buggy that was surprisingly easy to drive.

The layout of the garden was certainly beautiful, even though what should have been a flurry of colours in beds of various shapes were worn-out, drooping, sad little plants fighting for life. Some of the garden beds were circular and surrounded a stone table, the names of people etched into the side: 'Fanny Brew', 'Desmond Johns', 'Catalina Johns', 'Eleanor Johns' … many other Johns. Alex stopped to pay respect to the people she assumed were generations of the family who once lived in this place, and she ran her fingers along each of the letters.

When she happened upon one that read 'Edward Johns' she felt a shiver run down her spine and when she touched the letters of his name, her fingers sprang back in response to a little electric shock that buzzed through their tips. She put her hand to her heart and frowned. She stepped back slowly and looked around her. Blocked from the view of the house by a tall hedge, this one stood just next to the grand gazebo and Alex beheld it in awe. It seemed much bigger than when she'd rushed by it on her tour of the gardens the previous evening.

She guessed it was built in the mid-1900s. It was larger than any she'd seen in all her landscaping years and old-fashioned, with beams of steel scaffolding and cream-painted lattice that hung from the roof. The tiles that clung to the roof were grey and tattered, lichen worming their way through them. Alex could feel herself magnetised to the structure and as if in a dream, she floated towards it. She hesitated at its entrance and ran her fingers along the intricate designs that curved around the white posts and another shiver ran down her spine. Yet, she wasn't afraid; she mounted the four stone steps and apart from her heart, all she could hear were her boots clicking on the mahogany wooden boards. Her eyes raised themselves to the solid beams that held the ceiling so high and marvelled that without maintenance, which it was clearly devoid of, it still stood so tall, so erect, so majestic. She traced the steel rail with her fingers as she edged her way around it, admiring the neatly placed benches that surrounded almost the whole perimeter, until she was back where she started and she regretted having to leave it. Her foot hesitated on the second step and she turned back.

Before she knew what was happening, she could feel herself being drawn back into the gazebo and she stared at the floor as she walked, as if on air, to where the boards of wood met together in the middle, a circle of wood their base. She closed her eyes and raised her face to the ceiling, feeling herself lift to the tips of her toes; even with her work boots, she was able to balance on them, something she hadn't attempted in nearly fifteen years. She felt herself slowly spinning around and let whatever force moved her do its job, letting her mind float into oblivion, yet in that moment, she let a flash of her past nudge itself into her brain.

****

It was dark and the smell of rain permeated the air. Alex lay on the floor, sobbing, and she opened her eyes to see water rapidly pattering down outside the entrance of the gazebo which looked so far away. She squeezed her eyes shut and tried to work out how she ended up in this position, lying crouched on the floor, her arm around her knees. She let her eyes move about, fear enveloping her, but nothing moved, no other sound apart from the rain, drumming the roof with soft thuds. Her brain was cloudy, her back soaked with sweat and a sliver of terror held her frozen. For a moment she wondered where she was, and slowly put her hand to her mouth, trying to quell the sobs that came from it.

She squeezed her eyes closed again and shut out the sounds that distracted her and tried to recall what just happened.

A face, a man's face. She was close to him, could smell his scent, something old-fashioned, maybe soap, but different. A hand on her waist, pulling her to him. He was smiling, but his eyebrows were knitted; he looked concerned, he looked familiar. He was saying something, but she couldn't make out what. She was replying to him but she couldn't understand what she was saying, but she felt happy, didn't want him to go away.

A clap of thunder sounded and Alex jolted upright. She looked at her watch and suddenly realised where she was. Panic rose in her again; it was well past four thirty and the sun was high in the sky when she arrived at the steps of the gazebo. Milly had asked her to be back at the kitchen by one p.m., for lunch and she had missed it by hours. What had happened in the last four hours?

'Edward,' she said slowly and wondered where that had come from.

She sat up and felt an ache in her calves; she recognised it and swallowed hard. Taking a deep breath, she jumped up and shook herself, her arms, her legs, and wriggled her body, movements familiar to her, movements she hadn't made in a long time. She stopped suddenly and shook her head vigorously.

She got to her feet and headed shakily to the entrance, afraid to look behind her, and picked up her damp notebook, which had somehow landed on the ground outside. She opened her bottle of water and took a long swill, oblivious to the drops of rain that fell through her hair. She got into the golf cart and drove away, not allowing herself to think about what may have just happened. Then she looked at the gardens and cursed. She had hoped to spend the day completing her task of inventory. She had barely covered a quarter of the grounds. She'd even hoped to begin some work, or at least figure where the best place would be to start.

She pushed the incident out of her mind, she was an expert at doing that, and knew it was going to be a long first day.

CHAPTER 5

'We don't pay overtime,' said Rory with a twinkle in his eye when Alex came down the next morning. He was standing in the foyer, packing a laptop into his briefcase.

'Oh no. I don't expect …' Alex stuttered, wishing she could have just sneaked past, but the creaky stairs would have given her away anyway. She was on her way out to do her run, hoping that she would be able to find a good path which could become her morning routine.

'I'm teasing you,' he said, flicking his hand in front of his face.

'About what? The overtime?' Alex replied, grinning in defiance.

'Touché,' said Rory. 'But seriously, why were you working out there so late? It was dark when you came in.'

Alex wondered how he knew what time she'd come in.

The house was quiet, except for Milly packing up for the day in the kitchen, who scolded her for staying so late in the cold dark air. 'You will catch your death,' she said. 'It gets icy here, even in spring.'

'I … er, had to make a list of things I need to do and I had to figure where to start.'

'Yes, it is a big place.' He nodded and looked out the window. 'Did you work it out?'

For a second, Alex didn't realise what he was referring to, her mind had gone blank. She creased her brows in confusion.

'The place to start,' said Rory, his eyes imitating her own.

'Yeah, sorry. I'm acclimatising to things around here, I guess.' She reproached herself. He probably thought she was mad. 'I thought I should start from the driveway and work my way through the maze, from the left.'

He nodded again. 'Good idea,' he said absently and then looked at her and grinned. 'Sorry, it's all Greek to me, this gardening thing. Cathy was a little miffed you weren't here to tell you about her day. She wanted to go find you, but the rain came down and she thought you'd be back early, so she waited.'

'I'm sorry,' said Alex, unsure of how to feel. She couldn't

get close to anyone here. This was a job, very likely temporary. She was relieved Cathy didn't come looking for her. What a sight it would have been had she done so. What would she have seen? Alex now wished she had, then maybe Cathy could tell her what she'd been doing for those lost hours. She'd been struggling to retrieve from her brain what had happened and how she had landed on the floor in tears after all that time.

'Don't be, she was just excited. I'm sure she'll tell you all about it today.'

'Dad!' a voice from the top of the stairs called, a voice Alex had not heard before, and she saw the flicker of a frown cloud Rory's face.

'Netty,' he said, not necessarily to Alex, and putting down the briefcase, smiled apologetically at Alex and hurried up the stairs.

The mysterious other daughter, thought Alex, wondering when she would meet her.

'Going for a run, Milly,' she said as she hurried through the kitchen, not waiting for a response from the woman whose eyes were already raised in surprise. It was just past six thirty.

****

Alex developed her routine at the manor easily and stuck to it with furious determination. It was what kept her sane, what kept her mind from wandering to places they shouldn't … her parents, Nicholas … dancing. And it rarely varied, her alarm waking her at six a.m., when she jumped out of the warm bed into the cool room with a quick shower to shock her body into action. Then after, she threw on her track pants and sweater and took a run along the edge of the property, towards the shed, where she'd stop to nuzzle the horses, Quinn and Shoret, two beautiful brown beasts that now waited for her to whisper words of affection to them before she circled the perimeter of the property, by which time she was sweating and ready for another shower.

Then she'd head back to her room, change into her overalls and down to the kitchen where Milly already had an assortment of breakfast items, and Alex usually filled her cup with coffee and grabbed a scone on her way out. Then she'd haul the equipment she would need for the day into the golf cart and ride to the area on which she planned to work. At twelve-thirty, she lunched with Milly, while the cheery woman chattered on usually about the people at the market and the state of her sons' lives, and then she'd head back to work. At around five, the sun was already dipping, so there wasn't much more she could do; besides, Rory had told her she was fine to finish at around four.

She'd then have another shower, if she finished earlier, a bath, and dinner in the kitchen while the rest of the family ate in the dining room.

The rest of the evening was her own and Alex found she had time to do what she loved most, and that was to read. The house had a library, not as expansive as she had seen in old houses in old movies, but a size decent enough to keep her mind entertained forever if required.

'You can borrow whatever you want from here,' Rory had told her when he gave her a more thorough inspection of the house than Cathy had, the third day after her arrival.

'Wow,' said Alex, eyeing the rows and columns of books, wondering where to start.

Rory laughed. 'It's been organised into sections,' he said and she looked closely at the labels, running her fingers along the shelves, stopping at English – 1870s to 1950s and picking up *Great Expectations*.

'My favourite too,' said Rory. 'Good choice. It should keep you going for a while.'

'Thanks,' replied Alex and turned to leave.

'There's an alcove near the window with a beautiful view of the gardens, if you want to read in here.'

'Thanks,' Alex said again.

Rory peered at her in curiosity. 'You live her now, Alex. You can do what you want in this house. I don't need to give you permission.'

Alex wondered if Samuel felt the same but nodded and smiled in reply. Of course she never could feel that way in another person's home, but it was a nice gesture and she appreciated it.

Sundays were also her own and a week after she arrived at Lovelet Manor, Alex ventured into the town of Chernut, the main village, about twenty kilometres of winding roads from the house. Rory told her it was where he worked and where she may find some shops that were interesting. It didn't help that he said it with a dry voice and Alex was curious as to what the little town held.

As she moved past the gates of Lovelet Manor in her van, her breath caught in her throat and her chest became tight. It felt like what some people described as a panic attack, but Alex was cross with herself. There was nothing to be fearful of here and she took deep breaths to calm herself, wishing she had a paper bag from which she could breathe. She opened a window and the cool air caught her by surprise and she looked out the window to see a kangaroo hopping beside her. It was as if a calm hand had been placed on her chest and she smiled in relief, taking in the sounds of the bush, the intermittent call of the kookaburras, the trees that lined the lonely road swaying in greeting.

Maybe this is it. Maybe this is where I can use my inheritance, she thought, and the idea caused her hands to shake. No, she knew she couldn't touch that. She'd thought about it when she decided to leave Melbourne, but the decision to move had been too sudden and she needed to consider more carefully if it was the right decision. Frowning, she focused on the road ahead and was relieved when she saw a sign that announced the town of Chernut in the distance.

She parked her car at the centre of town, where a string of shops lay, and went into the newsagent, picking up a newspaper, the old woman at the counter eyeing her with some suspicion.

'I'm the Lovelet's gardener,' she said, wondering why she needed to reassure them she wasn't a threat.

The woman beamed. 'Rory is a wonderful man, isn't he? Teaches my son and he just loves him. So kind and thoughtful. Brayden, my son, talks about the man all the time, not like old Mrs Pouter. Doesn't like her.' She screwed up her nose.

'They are lovely,' said Alex, not quite knowing how to respond.

'The missus is a bit quiet. Only seen her a couple of times. Doesn't get out much.'

Alex, having put her money on the counter, was waiting for her change, but the woman clearly was in the mood for a chat. 'She's lovely too,' said Alex, wondering why she felt the need to defend a woman she had only met twice in the last week.

'I'll take your word for it.' The woman counted Alex's change and held on to it. 'Poor woman though. I feel sorry for them. What with that child.' She looked at Alex who got the feeling the woman was fishing for information, information Alex didn't have. She hadn't met Netty yet.

'Cathy's a sweet girl.'

The woman misunderstood. 'No, I meant the older one.' She raised her eyebrows.

'Yes,' said Alex and put her hand out for her change, which the woman reluctantly dropped coins into. 'Thank you. I'll see you maybe next week,' she said with a smile.

'Amber,' the woman called after her. 'My name's Amber.'

'Alexandra,' Alex replied, relishing the name that came from her lips.

As she left the newsagent, still amused by the old

woman's digging for dirt, she realised she would get much more information about the family for whom she worked than from the tight-lipped Milly, but she also realised she only needed to know what she needed to know. Their business was their own. She had never been in the habit of delving into other people's lives; after all, she hated when other people pried into hers.

She headed for the little shop that called itself a supermarket and felt the panic rise in her again, a feeling of unfamiliarity. She quickly bought some snacks that sat at the counter—two bags of chips, a bar of chocolate and mints—and rushed out, hoping the young attendant wouldn't be as talkative as the woman at the newsagency. He wasn't and she came out of the store feeling relief. It was little more than a week since she'd last entered a supermarket, busy as they were in Melbourne, and she never felt so closed in, so trapped. She tried to escape the feeling of panic that was trying to take hold of her by heading to what looked like a river, probably the same one she heard lapping in the silence of the night, and rested on a park bench, her sense of calm returning as she watched the ducks float by. She wondered what had caused her to panic. It wasn't as if she was like this all her life, certainly not before the accident, not really even after. Perhaps she felt exposed. But who on earth would even know who she was here? And who was she even escaping from? Nicholas. Would he look for her? Her heart told her yes, but her head disagreed. Yes, she was better off alone. Right now, all she wanted to do was get into her car and go back to Lovelet Manor where she felt safe.

As she entered the gates of the manor, she felt a calm
behold her and she let it envelop her, afraid of how she felt and
yet relieved. The word December popped into her head and she
hauled it out of her brain, focusing on the work there was to be
done. Even after a week, the gardens closest to the house looked
better, the azaleas that clung to the lattice on the house
welcoming her back. She smiled with relief and made a mental
note to touch up the shrubs near the window, which still looked a
little unkempt.

After that visit out of the grounds, Alex decided to make
her trips to town less often, perhaps once a month, and she spent
most Sundays exploring the bushland over the garden walls,
where miles and miles of green and brown landscape made her
feel like she was home. Beyond that, she could see a wooded area
where the sound of water could be heard. She intended to
explore more of the area and decided that Sundays were the days
she would, no more venturing out of the walls unless it was
absolutely necessary.

She knew she was already in love with this place, where
nothing was expected of her, except for the beautification of the
gardens, judged only by a resentfully pleased Samuel, who visited
every second Sunday evening to inspect the place. The pace was
so much slower than Melbourne and she loved the serenity, often
going for walks in the evening, keeping to the fence for fear of

losing her way somewhere in the big, wide-open fields.

At times, she'd sit on a garden bench, careful to avoid even facing the gazebo, wary of its magnetism. She couldn't lose time again to an imaginary man, as lovely as he smelled. She'd have to get herself committed! She had avoided the gazebo since that first day, hoping she could put off tending to that section of the gardens for as long as possible, but she couldn't dispel the feeling that something was calling her back and she resisted glancing in its direction. But Alex had never felt more content, something she hadn't felt in a long time, something that was wonderful and yet unnerving.

CHAPTER 6

'Mummy is with Netty,' said Cathy, walking by Alex's side, holding a little watering can and pouring drops of water onto the petals of the flowers she passed. She looked up at Alex. 'Have you seen Netty?'

'No,' said Alex. It had been nearly four weeks and she'd still not met the girl whose home was her room. Alex saw the balcony on the second floor, usually uninhabited, the door that led to the room always covered with a curtain. She wondered if the girl ever came out of there.

'Why not?'

'I don't know.' Alex couldn't tell her she hadn't been invited to meet her sister. The little girl wouldn't understand.

'She was mean to me today,' said Cathy in a small voice.

Alex kept her head towards the ground. 'Oh?'

'I don't think she wanted to be. But I sometimes think

she doesn't like me.'

'Well, I'm sure that's not true.'

'I know she likes me.' She hesitated. 'But …'

Alex turned to face Cathy and the girl looked into her eyes, tears sitting on the brim of her eyes.

'Sometimes Mummy doesn't like me.'

'Oh no, Cathy,' said Alex, taking the girl's soft, clean hand in her own grubby ones. 'Your mum loves you. Don't even think that way.'

'No, I know she does, but just not all the time.'

'Your mother has a lot on her plate,' said Alex, wondering just what it was, but it was the right thing to say.

'Yeah, she's always busy with Netty, but.'

'Your sister isn't well.'

'I hope she doesn't die.'

Alex didn't know how to reply to this, so she pointed to the rose bush nearby. 'Hey, can you help me? I forgot to water that bush. Can you put some on there for me?'

Cathy's face broke out in a smile. 'Yes.' She skipped away.

Alex sighed. She didn't know whether she was supposed to distract her or let the little girl talk out her fears. She was no child psychologist, but distraction seemed to be the best option at the time, particularly when she didn't exactly know what was wrong with the sister, but if she was to have these conversations with the sensitive little girl, she'd better find out soon.

She felt sorry for Cathy; the usually quiet, almost eerie house would come alive when she got home from school, and if Alex wasn't indoors, the little girl, her pigtails flying behind her, would run into the gardens to look for her, so she could tell her about her day at school, her teachers, her friends and her work. She had taken a liking to Alex almost immediately and Alex enjoyed the ramblings of the little girl, who was so animated, so vibrant; she reminded her of herself when she was that age, in a time when things were simple and fun.

Cathy sometimes found her curled up in the library and she'd prop herself next to Alex, who offered to read her a story and let the little girl crawl in to the crook of her arm while she read about faraway lands, fairies, beasts and outer space. Alex could see this girl was quite alone, with Cheryl not having a lot of time to dote on her younger daughter, who'd often spend time in the kitchen with Milly or out in the garden with Scamper the old dog, who could barely do as his name implied. Alex was growing fond of the little girl, even though she knew she shouldn't; she couldn't, knowing she may break her heart and have her own broken in the process, should she have to leave.

May 27

Dear Mum and Pa,

It's been more than a month and I'm sorry I haven't had time to talk. I've been so busy here, but this is going to be a long one! So I'll start with the odd man who hired me. I don't see much of him because he doesn't live here—thank God for that. Anyway, he's a bit strange, but nothing I can't deal with. Then there's the couple who are also a bit weird. He seems fine, but a bit sad; the wife though, she looks a bit like a ghost, just wanders around. I haven't quite worked her out yet, but I haven't talked to her much really. I can't explain it; she seems nice, but she has this faraway look, like she's always somewhere else. It could be because of the daughter I haven't met yet, which is weird because we all live in the same house! Anyway, this daughter is sick, I don't know what it is, but it must be bad if she has to stay in her room all the time. The other one, Cathy, she's cute. She showed me around when I first got here. Oh Ma! If you saw this place, not just the house with this gigantic library, which I think you would love, but the gardens! I sometimes think I've died and gone ... You would love it. I remember our own garden and I try to make this one look like yours. Anyway, it's really what I think I needed. Oh, and there's Milly. You'd like Milly, but I thought she would be more of a gossip. I've learned nothing from her, but I don't need to anyway; as you always said, Dad, mind your own business, not everyone else's. So I better go now, my eyes are closing. Oh, and I've been able to put him out of my mind, so I think I'll be okay. Love you both, xx.

It was to be the very next day when Alex met Netty. After a long day of work, where she'd had to dig a deep ditch along the side of a stone path, to let water flow through to the lilacs, Alex intended to have a shower and go for a walk to enjoy the setting of the sun when a sudden downpour literally dampened her plans. She didn't mind the alternative though, curling up with a book in the bath until the water grew cold—which book, she hadn't decided; she was devouring three at the same time.

When she heard the word 'mother' called out tentatively, as she ascended the stairs, she paused on the landing, knowing well that Cheryl was in the kitchen with Cathy cajoling her into eating the broccoli she had left on her dinner plate. Rory was rarely at home, so Alex wondered whether she should respond. She decided not to; after all, she had been there for more than a month and there had been no move from Cheryl or Rory to introduce her to the other daughter, one that clearly stayed in her room and had some health problem that she had no clue about. Even Milly didn't attempt to enlighten her, and Alex didn't want to ask about it as it was none of her business.

As she stepped forward, the board beneath her creaked and she hear the cry again, this time more doggedly. She followed to where the voice emanated and found herself in front of a white door, adorned with the name 'Annette' in large swirling font, slightly ajar.

She knocked softly.

'Come,' said the voice, now small, unsure.

Alex pushed the door open slowly and saw a young girl, a face full of make-up, sitting on a king-size bed. Two tables sat on one side and another on the right, with an array of things on them, from make-up palettes to books, magazines and a games console. The girl, who Alex surmised was about ten or eleven years old, opened her eyes wide at the sight of Alex and shrunk back into her pillow. She was the spitting image of her mother, except that her face was coloured like a clown. Alex could see she was frightened and held up her hand.

'I'm Alex,' she said and stood with her hand remaining on the handle of the door. 'You must be Netty.'

The girl nodded and pulled her blanket up over her chest, covering a cotton nightgown.

'I'm the new landscaper.' She knew how silly it would sound to a young girl meeting a strange woman in her room, calling herself a landscaper. 'Your parents hired me to … er … tidy up the gardens.' Netty still stared, her large eyes fearful, and Alex stepped back. It must have been scary to a young child to see a stranger with mud all over her clothes at her bedroom door. She patted her unruly hair to help the image even though she knew it would make no difference to the unruly curls that had a mind of their own. 'I heard you call out. Do you need something?'

Netty shook her head and Alex backed out of the room.

'Alex?'

Alex turned back to Netty, whose hands had let go of the blanket now. 'Yes?'

'Can you help me take this off my face?'

Alex thought it was a strange request but smiled and went to the side of the bed. 'How old are you, Netty?'

'Fourteen.'

Wow. Much older than she thought. 'Well, Netty, when you apply make-up, you should really consider when taking tips from the mascot of McDonald's.'

The girl's eyebrows raised and Alex wondered if she had overstepped, but in a moment Netty was laughing, a shrill laugh that ended in a rasping cough. She leaned forward and Alex didn't know what to do so she rubbed her back awkwardly until Netty leaned back on her pillow.

'Let's see here,' said Alex, rummaging through the make-up, looking for something to wipe the muck off Netty's face. She found some wet wipes and softly began to smooth the foundation from the young girl's face, carefully rubbing off the bright red lipstick that seemed to have missed its mark completely. Then Netty closed her eyes while Alex removed the streaks of mascara from her eyelids. 'There,' said Alex, satisfied that all traces of make-up were now staining the wipes.

'Thank you,' said Netty when Alex put the last of the wipes in the bin. 'I got the make-up for my birthday, but I just tried it and … well.' She picked up the handheld mirror and looked at her face and Alex saw the image of Cheryl, the pale white skin, the dark eyebrows, the jet-black hair, that cascaded to her waist. The girl looked despondently at her reflection and Alex felt her heart cry a little, and again wondered what exactly was wrong with her.

'Do you want me to help?' Alex ventured.

Netty spun her head towards Alex. 'Would you?'

'Sure,' said Alex, not really so sure. She was certainly no expert in make-up, but she did know how to make herself look decent when the very rare occasion afforded it. She thought about her smeared mascara when she first arrived here and suppressed a giggle.

She gently applied a thin layer of foundation, a soft beige palette of eyeshadow, black mascara flicked lightly on the lashes that didn't seem to need any, and a shimmer of lip gloss, while Netty remained still, her eyes on Alex's chin.

'There, have a look,' said Alex when she was done and handed Netty the mirror.

'Wow,' Netty whispered and blinked. 'Thank you.'

'You're welcome,' said Alex and began to pack away the mess that Netty had made. 'I would reconsider taking tips from the Kardashians from now on,' she said, nodding towards a magazine that was open to a page of some very heavily made-up women. She stood up. 'Okay, well, I'll see you later,' she said, not knowing what to say. She wasn't even sure if she was allowed to meet this girl, let alone paint her face. She hoped Cheryl and Rory wouldn't be upset.

As she rose from the edge of the bed, Netty grabbed her hand. 'It's Annette,' she said. 'My name. Can you call me that? It's more grown up than Netty.'

'Yes, sure, Annette,' replied Alex with a smile, remembering what it was like to be fourteen and removing the thought from her mind again.

'And can you come back sometimes, not just to fix my face, but you know ...'

Alex didn't want to make promises about things that she wasn't sure of but the earnestness on the face of the girl made her nod.

She went back to her room, retrieved *The Outsiders* and

headed for the bathroom, but she couldn't concentrate, the look of the girl still on her mind, the frail fingers that gripped the mirror, the gaunt features of her face, the room that seemed to have everything a teenager could possibly want …

May 28

Dear Mum and Pa,

I met the other daughter, Netty. Oh, I almost cried. I don't think she can move her legs, and she seems very weak, even the way she talks, so soft. I still don't know what her problem is, but she's so young and innocent and so fragile. But I see something of myself in her, and it's like I want to help her to be okay with herself. She just wants to be a regular teenager, but she can't. I don't know why they don't take her out of the room. I must ask. I could wheel her through the gardens, maybe take her to the horses or something. I don't know, it's not my place anyway.

I've been thinking about my episode, the one from the day after I arrived. I hope it was just a one-off, but nothing has happened since. I don't go past the gazebo anymore. It gives me the heebie-jeebies. I hate that I lost time, I was a bit worried about it, but maybe it's because I saw the dance hall and that freaked me out. I am trying to avoid things that remind me of the past, but then something unexpected happens and I feel like I'm going backwards. I wish I could talk to you both in person, you would understand.

Love and miss you xx

****

She stroked the stalk, trying to love it back to life, but she knew this one was a goner. The stem was already brittle and the ground it tried to emerge from was as hard as a rock. She tugged at it and fell on her bottom as it gave way and broke from the shoot.

'How are you doing?'

Alex looked up to see Cheryl standing before her trying to mask a giggle, one hand atop her hat to keep it from flying away with the breeze, and the other holding out a basket.

'I'm doing okay,' Alex replied, shielding her eyes from the sunlight and admiring the face trying to come to life with that snicker. She wished she would just let it out; what a beautiful face that would be. 'Thanks.' She got up and took the basket, the smell of cold meats making her mouth water, and moved to the bench that sat next to the garden. It seemed there were more benches in this garden than garden.

'Okay,' said Cheryl and swayed hesitantly.

Alex dusted her hands on her overalls and sat down, opening the basket. She was hungry; it had been a warm day and

71

she hadn't stopped for lunch. She had missed going in for lunch on several occasions. Finding a cloth inside, she wiped her hands again and pulled out a wicker tray that contained salami, cheese, ham and a miniature French-stick.

'I did it myself,' said Cheryl uncertainly and Alex moved along the bench to make room for her.

'Nice,' she said. 'Share it with me. There's too much here for me anyway.'

Cheryl didn't move, but a crooked smile, tentative, fearful, crossed her face. She looked towards the main house. 'I have to get back to Netty,' she said. 'Maybe another time?'

'Sure,' replied Alex, wondering about this beautiful, strange creature who just seemed to wander about the house aimlessly. 'I met your other daughter yesterday,' she said, feeling like she was admitting guilt. 'I helped her with some makeup. I hope that's okay.'

'Oh yes,' replied Cheryl, who seemed to be relieved that it was Alex who brought it up. 'She told me. Of course, it's okay. She likes you. She talked about you the whole of yesterday evening.'

'She's lovely,' said Alex. She had the feeling that this was Cheryl's way of urging her back to the girl's room. 'If you like, I could stop in to see her every now and then?'

'Yes, that would be nice,' said Cheryl, her eyes lighting up. 'She would love that; only if you have time and want to.'

'Yes, of course, I'd love to.' Alex thought it was strange that there had been no attempt to introduce her to Cheryl's daughter, but now she was suddenly urging her to. She held up the piece of bread. 'Thanks again.'

Cheryl gave a shy wave and turned to go.

'Hey, Cheryl.' Alex wasn't sure if she should mention anything yet.

'Yes?' Cheryl turned around, almost too quickly, and Alex realised this woman must be lonely. It was best not to question her about anything right now. Not December, not the gazebo. It could wait.

'Are you sure you don't want to stay, just for a bit?'

The smile was surer now, warm and genuine, and it lit up her face, her grey eyes almost piercing. 'Maybe for a minute.' She looked around her, fingering the stalks on the heliconia, and sighed.

Alex wasn't sure how to start a conversation with her, so she bit on the bread and stuffed a folded piece of salami in her mouth. Maybe Cheryl would begin.

It seemed to work. 'It's so beautiful here. I don't want to

leave,' said Cheryl.

'Why would you leave?' puffed out Alex, swallowing her food to keep Cheryl talking.

'Because it's time to go.'

'Where?' asked Alex and wondered if she were being too nosy. But she realised that this move would affect her too. It was her business too and not a word had been said about it since Samuel had mentioned it on the day she'd arrived.

'We don't know yet. Maybe Melbourne ...' She looked at Alex, as if just noticing her there. 'Hey, you're from Melbourne, aren't you? I heard Sam tell Rory.' Her eyes glowed again. 'What's it like?' She plopped herself on her haunches so close in front of Alex, Alex had to rear back.

'Like every other city, I guess. Noisy, busy, never stops.' She gazed at the gardens. 'I have never had so much peace since I've been here.' She meant it. She slept all night, every night since her arrival, soundly. It hadn't been that way in a long time. There was just something ... 'Have you lived here for long?'

'For too long, but I never tire of it. I'm trying to get excited about moving but ...' The haze had clouded Cheryl's eyes again and she stood up. 'I have to go. I hope you enjoy the food.'

'It's great, thanks,' said Alex and watched as Cheryl

turned to leave, staring after the retreating figure, a feeling of sorrow enveloping her.

CHAPTER 7

She dreamt about him that night. She couldn't exactly remember the details, but she was searching and yelling, something she rarely did, and his face, serene, smiling kept fading when she got near enough to touch him. When she woke, her face flushed and her back in a pool of sweat, she was angry with herself. Angry she'd let herself even dream about him. She had been so successful in keeping him out of her mind, she was sure she was close to erasing the memory of him from her brain. She threw off the covers and shivered, the wet of her back soaking in the cold air, and she hunched on the side of the bed, her feet cold and her palms warm.

Nicholas.

She slid to the floor and tugged at the unopened suitcase, drawing it out from under the bed where it had remained since she got here, more than two weeks ago.

Her mouth was dry and she licked her lips, looking at the

empty jug of water mocking her from her nightstand. She threw it an angry glance and ran her fingers along the zipper of the suitcase, daring herself to open it. Just one look wouldn't hurt.

His smile danced up at her and she held the frame close to her face, her thumb following the line between his eyebrows down to his nose, pausing at the little bump which he complained about.

'That's why I don't play football anymore,' he had said with a frown.

Alex had laughed. 'You're a vain man!'

'Well, there's that, and really, that's a good excuse. I just wasn't any good.' He'd chuckled.

She let her hand run over his cheek, feeling the warmth it exuded through the cold glass, and she felt a tear slide down the side of her face, ignoring the ramming at her brain, telling her to put the picture back, to keep ignoring the temptation to think about him. But she ignored her head and let her heart command her. He deserved at least that.

'Nicholas,' she said softly.

Nicholas, the man she gave eight years of her life to, and yet she knew it was not giving. Not nearly the same as he had. The past had tormented her and still tried to and she let it beat her.

But when she met Nicholas, she thought she had won, that she could overcome the anguish, the grief that held her locked out from the world around her. She remembered when she first set eyes on him, crouched beside an artificial pond, swirling something powdery in the water, when the assistant announced her presence. He shook his hands of the droplets and stood up. Lanky. That was the word that first came to her mind. Then he turned to her and his big brown eyes creased, a smile almost involuntarily filling his face. In that moment, the tension she'd felt from the moment she called to apply for the job, two days before, vanished.

Even as she walked into the nursery, the greenery, the smell of freshly cut flowers had almost choked her as thoughts of her mother flooded her mind. She had already been second-guessing her decision: it would be too hard, too familiar, too painful. But now, as she looked at this man who was rambling over, tucking a glove into the back pocket of his jeans, she felt an unfamiliar feeling, a desperate need to do well in this interview, to get this job, to be around him. She let her usual need for self-preservation slip and she caught herself. She couldn't get involved with anyone, and who was she kidding? Why would anyone want to be around her anyway? A shy, crazy-haired recluse, who had still not gotten rid of the baggage she'd carried for years.

'Hey, there,' he said approaching her. 'You must be

Blanche.'

'Yes, that's me,' she responded, hating the sound of her name.

'Well, come on,' he said, wiping his hands on his jeans, his eyes as smiling as his lips.

She fell in love with him on the spot and not thirty minutes later, had the job.

Nicholas was a man with a laugh so hearty, it was odd to hear it come from someone so scrawny, and with a heart so big, he reminded her of her father and the grudge she felt for him leaving her began to wane. Nicholas made her laugh and she didn't feel guilty for laughing, she didn't feel the pain that pierced her heart every time she thought of them. She even let him soothe her when something took her off guard, like a dandelion in the wind, or a sight of a Gunnera, the large leaves of which she'd use to shelter her when a sudden burst of rain fell from the sky, the same ones she'd use to hide behind when she was called in for dinner.

When Nicholas came into her life, she began to let herself remember them, the fun things, scrambling to get to the car, while she waited for them, tapping her foot loudly on the floor, alerting them of their tardiness, her mother with toast still sticking out of her mouth, her father still locking his briefcase. They'd both turn to face her in the back seat with screwed-up faces and Alex could not help but laugh at their silliness. She thought of the trips to the beach, not far from where they lived, her parents rushing into the water, dragging her with them, insisting in this country, she couldn't afford to be afraid of the water. And she wasn't. She was one of the best swimmers in her school, taking out the blue ribbons at all the swimming carnivals. She remembered their smiles, their laughs, even the way they scolded her for whatever reason, never angry with her for long.

And she remembered the way they danced. When she crept out of her bed at night, the soft lull of music drawing her out of her room, where she watched them through the bars of the banister, his arms around her, her face looking up to his, their movements so familiar, so smooth, so intimate.

That all disappeared on that fateful night. The life she'd depended on, no, taken for granted, vanished in the glare of a car's headlights and since then, Alex lived a life of dull grey. Such a cliché. *My parents died in a car accident.* It sounded made up, like she was desperate for attention, for pity.

The two years between that night and her high-school graduation, when she moved to a little suburban flat, she preferred not to think about. The time she lived with her aunt and so-called uncle, who treated her with disdain for the most part, except when they discussed her inheritance. The weird little stares he gave her, the brushes past her when her aunt wasn't around … and then finally when he made his move. This was the time she resented her parents, not giving them a moment of her thought. She didn't grieve for them, she hated them for leaving her with these people.

Alex was not a stupid girl and even at sixteen, it was obvious what they were after and why they took her in, but it would be over her dead body that she'd give them anything that was left to her by her parents, try as they did to cry poverty to her, even going so far as to suggest she was a burden to them, for all of the two years she was left with them.

Her father had been a wise man, leaving everything they owned, including the large house in the leafy green suburb of Parkdale, to his only daughter, who, when she turned eighteen, asked for it to be sold. Mr Sidebottom, her father's lawyer, who checked on Alex every couple of months while she was living with her aunt and uncle, was surprised.

'I thought you'd want to stay there. The lease on the house is nearly up.'

But it was not a place Alex wanted to be without them and living there would only bring back memories of happier times, times she knew she would never have again. 'No. I want to move out on my own. I will keep the job at the café and I think it will be enough. Mr Roberts has given me a full-time position now that school is done.'

'But what will you do with the money?'

'Just keep it where it is?' Alex screwed up her face. She didn't know if that were possible.

'There's already a substantial amount in there,' said Mr Sidebottom incredulously. 'You don't want to use it for something?'

'I don't need anything.'

'Most eighteen-year-olds would shop till they dropped,' said the old man, twisting his little goatee in puzzlement.

Alex looked down at her jeans. She could certainly use a good shopping trip, but the thought of spending her parents' money on frivolous things made her uneasy.

'Well, you have a good mind for money, Blanche.' He nodded and gathered his papers that were strewn on Aunt Helen's dining table.

Alex didn't want to tell him she was scared to touch it, scared to spend it away and have nothing to show for the existence of her parents.

'Well, without the sale of the house, there is …'

'I don't want to know,' Alex cut in. She'd rather not be tempted.

'But …'

'I trust you, Mr Sidebottom …'

'Tom.'

Alex couldn't call this man Tom. She'd known him all her life, he was like a jolly uncle who popped into their house for a bourbon with her father, often bringing Alex a knick-knack from his office. She never really called him anything, and never realised it until now. And she did trust him. Her father certainly had.

'More coffee, Tom?' Aunt Helen strolled into the kitchen and Alex clenched her teeth. She knew she had been listening the whole time.

Mr Sidebottom cringed at the sound of his name coming from this woman's lips and clicked the lock on his briefcase. 'No, thank you. I think we're done.' He stood up and walked to the door. 'I'll let you know when it sells,' he whispered to Alex. 'Call me if you need anything,' he said more loudly, making sure Aunt Helen heard that.

'Why are you keeping it all in there?' Aunt Helen pounced as soon as Alex shut the door, and Alex was sure Mr Sidebottom had heard her from outside.

'What? The house?'

'I didn't know you were going to sell it.'

'I don't want it.'

'What about the money? Did he tell you how much there is?'

'No.'

'Why not? What sort of lawyer is he?'

Alex sighed and wished it were already next month. Her birthday was the day she would move. She'd already arranged a flat, as bare as it would be. 'I didn't ask.'

'Well, you are nearly an adult, missy, you can't keep just living here, rent free.'

Alex thought it was about the right time to tell her aunt about her plans. 'I'm moving out next month. On my birthday.'

Aunt Helen's eyebrows shot up and she stepped back like she had been stung. 'And when were you going to tell me?'

Alex felt guilty. She'd known for a while but had only arranged it last week while at work. 'Well, now, I guess.'

'And what about us?'

'Thank you for looking after me,' Alex felt obliged to say.

'Ungrateful,' Aunt Helen spat. 'Now that you have money, you don't want to stay with us anymore.'

Alex didn't want to tell her she never wanted to stay here, the courts made her, but she felt a sliver of guilt nevertheless. 'I'm happy to ask Mr Sidebottom to reimburse you for your trouble.'

'That's all *you've* been, trouble,' said the woman and walked away.

Alex sighed and wished the money never existed. She had no inclination to use any of it and the thought of buying another house with it pierced her heart more deeply than going back to live in the house she had loved—with their ghosts.

She trudged to her job at the café every day and spent her evenings trying to make things grow in the little pots on the kitchen windowsill of her flat. She wished she could have a garden but knew it would be some time before she could move into a bigger place. It certainly wasn't feasible with the money she was making. She tried to look at places to buy, houses that her parents would like for her to live in, but search as she may, nothing was good enough and she realised she may never find what she was looking for. But Alex was happy by herself, with no one to tell her she was in the way and no one who threw her lascivious glances.

And she reconnected with her parents.

She found herself alone and the pain in her chest made her want to cry. The school had tried to give her counselling, but she could never explain to them how she felt, how lost she was and how she wished she had gone with them that night. No, she held her head high and told them she was coping, that her aunt and uncle were helping her cope—she had learned how to lie, even to herself. But living by herself, with nothing to think about, and no one to answer to, Alex had too much time on her hands, and there was only so much reading she could do. She ran every morning and read at night, but when she put down her book, the pounding in her heart became too much and one night she sat up in bed, pummelled her fists on the bedcovers and screamed in frustration.

'Why? Why did you go?'

It was as if a heavy stone had been lifted from her chest, and she continued to talk to them. 'I miss you so much. Are you there? In Heaven? Are you with me? I still think you have to be here, somewhere, it's like you can't be gone.'

She opened the bedside drawer and took out her notepad. 'You're not gone,' she said. 'You're just away.'

She began to scribble. *'Dear Mum and Pa ...'*

Since then as she wrote them, sometimes daily, sometimes weekly, packing them into yearly bunches, she felt better. She was still talking to them, even though they couldn't talk back, but she felt a peace that she hadn't before. They were still with her.

Then one New Year's Eve, three years later, after explaining her day to them, she was about to pack the letters together and tie them with a string when, out of curiosity, she opened the first one she had written for the year. And as she read, she realised that the content was almost the same as the one she had just written. She read them all, twenty-eight in the year, sometimes a few lines telling of her day, sometimes long, drawn-out letters telling them how much she missed them. Of course, there were the odd bits of news: David, the man who came into her life and left it just as quickly; Mary from the café who had the same problems with the manager, Mark, who asked her out, and who she'd refused because he was too nice, but in essence, there wasn't much to say. She couldn't tell them how much her feet itched to dance, how much she wanted to blast the music and let it hold her as it used to; she refused to think about what used to be, what could never be anymore, and her guilt could never be explained in words.

If her parents were really receiving these letters, they would be so disappointed with her, languishing in her comfortable state, a life going nowhere, a job she went to because it was something to do. She packed away the bundle with a new resolve. She was going to do something she loved to do. If she didn't have relationships, that was fine, she chose not to, but she could at least have something she looked forward to, something to make her life a little more meaningful.

It seemed like fate, as when she opened the paper the next morning, an advertisement for a salesperson at Hortitech, a garden store three blocks from her flat, jumped out at her.

And that was where she met Nicholas that very first day. Nicholas was the owner and had a number of people in his employ, and Alex enjoyed going to work with him always close by, teaching her the tricks of the trade, chatting to her on her lunch break. And she felt close to her parents, thought about them often, talked to them about her work, sometimes out loud.

'These fuchsias are stunning. I don't think we had these. I can't remember,' Alex said, trying to picture the pink flowers in her childhood garden.

'Did you say something?' Alex jumped and turned around to see Nicholas standing at the end of the greenhouse. His lip was curled in a teasing smile. It was only a couple of months after she had begun working at Hortitech and he had caught her chattering away to nobody on more than a few occasions.

'No. Sorry,' Alex replied, feeling like her face must match her hair.

Nicholas walked over. 'You do that a lot.'

Alex reddened more. 'Do I?' she asked sheepishly.

Nicholas nodded. 'Who do you talk to?' He winked. 'A

long-lost lover?'

'No, nothing like that,' she said hurriedly.

'A present lover?' He was not grinning anymore.

Alex felt her heart skip. 'No present lover.' Alex thought of the few men she'd dated. She always found fault with them; they drank too much, they wanted too much from her, they didn't want enough of her … She tired of men quickly and felt no lasting grief when the relationship ended.

Nicholas nodded, tried not to smile and walked away.

It was a year later when he finally got the courage to ask her on a date and three months later when she finally accepted. It wasn't as if she wasn't attracted to men, she'd had her share of flings, but nothing stuck. But with Nicholas, she knew he was not going to be a fling. He was the first man that tapped at her heart the moment she saw him. She knew she could fall for him and just the thought of being hurt, of losing something she may grow attached to, scared her silly. That's why it took so long for her to accept his date. Later she would put it down to happiness and the fact that it would never last. She had been happy, for sixteen years of her life, and she knew it was fleeting, and devastating. She couldn't go through that again.

He never pushed for information about her past and she appreciated his discretion. Before Nicholas, she didn't know whether she would ever be able to share with anyone what happened and she didn't have anyone to share it with, so Nicholas was a breath of fresh air that blew into her cloistered life.

She loved Nicholas the moment she saw him and fell in love with him more every day she spent with him. When he touched her, she shivered, when he kissed her, she felt weak and she knew this was going to break her heart. The intensity of their first few years tempered to a oneness that she'd never experienced before. And slowly, she found herself unravelling, in the best and worst way possible. She told him of her parents, of the two years with her aunt and uncle, and of the loneliness she'd felt since her parents left her.

'I can't understand what you've been through,' said Nicholas, whose own family lived in Cairns, and whom he had a meagre relationship with. 'But I know I won't ever leave you alone.'

Alex had nodded but she wasn't so sure. She knew he loved her, but so had her parents. She still wrote to them and was glad she had something to tell them, something that was new and exciting.

... but I'm scared. He may leave, he may ... I love him so much, it's not like anything I've felt before, not even close. And I know he loves me.

He asked again last night. I don't know what to say anymore. I can't say yes. It's been four years and I still can't get used to how much he loves me. I wish you could tell me what to do. Give me a sign.

Love and miss you.

The signs never came and after years of proposals and negative responses, Nicholas had had enough. She refused to move in with him, insisting what they had was enough for them.

'Why won't you even move in with me? We spend every night together anyway. It's a waste to pay rent when you can move into my place.'

'That's not the point.'

'Then what is?'

Alex was silent. She didn't want to tell him she was waiting for the worst to happen. But yet she didn't want to lose him.

'But I want to spend my life with you. I want children.'

'I don't,' she replied, not so sure, but unwilling to submit.

'Why won't you marry me?'

'Because …'

'Yes, I know, the way things are is enough for you.' He'd frowned.

'Then maybe it's time to end this,' she'd said, almost relieved that this was being taken out of her hands.

'No,' he cried. 'Why are you doing this?'

'Because we want different things.'

'You can't mean that.'

But she did. And she told him to leave. And he'd left. And there was nothing there for her in Melbourne anymore. She had to go away, far away, put him out of her mind and feel no temptation to go to him. She phoned in to work and left a message with Jenny, the receptionist, telling her she had to take a few days off. When he didn't call her the next day or the day after, she began to pack her things into her minivan and checked the want ads.

She knew it was fate again when the first thing she set her eyes on was a position in Chernut, a town four hours from Melbourne. It was time to move on.

****

She swiped at her cheeks, pushing away the tears that now fell down her face and onto his picture. She wiped at the glass with the end of her sleeve, put the picture back in the suitcase and slid it under the bed again. There was no turning back.

I dreamt about him last night, I don't know why. I've tried not to think about him and it's worked so far. I miss you, goodnight.

CHAPTER 8

The days drifted in and out without incident and soon the grey umbrella of winter covered the manor, its tentacles taking with it the glory of the garden, reducing the walkways to a mushy sop, and Alex trudged the grounds every day in her gumboots, trying to avoid sliding in the mud. But she worked the days as she always did, beginning early after her morning run and finishing at four thirty, enjoying nourishing the plants back to life and relishing the thought of spending the dreary evenings in the library reading.

She saved all her money, for what she didn't know yet, but there wasn't anything she needed or wanted, apart from personal items which she shopped for each month, when she forced herself off the grounds of the mansion. She was getting used to the little town, enjoying her chats with the nosy but sweet Amber, the woman at the newsagent, who told her of the gossip in town, about people Alex had never met. Lily, the daughter of the mayor, who ran off with a lout who had come through town on his hotted-up Harley-Davidson, the oldest woman in town, Carrie-Ann, who had just passed away a week before her hundredth birthday and other tidbits of information she shared with Alex, who smiled and nodded, allowing the woman to chat. After she'd torn herself away from Amber, she'd go to the supermarket where she usually brought back a treat for herself and also for Cathy and a magazine for Annette. From there she'd amble over to the river and watch the ducks flit about on the water, enjoying the simplicity of this life, wondering why she hadn't thought to move into the country sooner. Then she'd get into her car and head home.

Cathy would fling open the door and smile patiently while Alex retrieved her treat from her shopping bag and would receive a hug around the legs for it. Then she'd head up to Annette's room and listen for any sound of life and if she did, she'd give her the magazine and if she didn't, she'd tiptoe in and drop it on her bed, if Annette was asleep. Every Monday and Thursday, a cache of medical people came to the house, and stayed for half the day. For the rest of those evenings, Cheryl was nowhere to be seen, Cathy followed Alex around like a lost puppy, and Rory sat in his armchair, a forlorn look on his face and an ignored book on his lap. There was never to be any good news. Her state, as Alex finally found out from Cheryl, was a type of cancer, a degenerative disease that was in its final stages.

Alex visited Annette's room on occasion, usually when

Cheryl asked her to check in on her, or when she hadn't done so in a while and thought the girl may need a different face. Angela, her regular nurse, only came in during the afternoon and Annette didn't want much to do with the woman who she complained 'nagged at her'. Alex was happy to help out, knowing Cheryl needed a break, and often watched a movie with Annette or talked to her of books, introducing her to Enid Blyton, probably a little too childish for someone of Annette's age, but she still enjoyed them too, so she read aloud while Annette listened, sometimes dozing off.

'Why don't you go out into the balcony?' Alex asked her one day, seeing the curtains spread open, a touch of sunshine streaming through the windowpane.

Annette screwed up her face and shrugged.

Alex walked over to the curtains and looked out. She gasped. The view from Annette's room was dazzling. She had wondered why Annette's room was on the second floor, but now she could see why. She felt a little stab of pride as she looked over the work she had done, the area to the left of the window bright and colourful, neat and manicured, the other side, which she had not yet gotten to, a little worse for wear. Then her eyes fell upon the gazebo and the familiar tingle ran down her spine. 'So, why don't you?' said Alex opening the door and stepping into the spacious balcony which was adorned with two chairs and a table, and plenty of space for Annette's bed to be wheeled out. She knew by now that Annette couldn't move her legs, that the bed she lay in almost all day was designed to help her muscles, to keep the pain at bay, that it was only in absolute agony that Annette could leave the bed.

'I don't know. I don't like it.' Annette folded her arms and turned the other way.

'Okay,' said Alex, not wanting to push her. 'But there's nothing like fresh air to …'

'You have to like it. You're the gardener.'

Alex felt stung but tried to understand why the girl wouldn't like to go out. She was still trapped, still a prisoner in the bed in which she lay, and seeing the world to where she would never go would be disheartening. 'Sure, I get it.' Alex smiled. 'Enjoy the mag.'

'Thanks,' muttered Annette and Alex closed the door behind her, feeling the same sense of doom whenever she left the girl. As soon as she walked back into the garden, Scamper at her feet, Alex felt her heart lighten. It was Sunday and her day off, but Alex still walked through the paths, picking at bits of weeds she found worming their way through the plants, neatening up the place she took pride in now.

She spent most of her evenings walking through the gardens, enjoying the freedom she felt, nothing binding her to anything, the choice to do whatever she wanted and go wherever she wished. She'd been there nearly two months and already she was beginning to make some headway in the keeping of the gardens. There was a long way to go, but it was already looking decent and her view from the balcony assured her she was doing her job.

'My my,' she said to the camellias. 'You guys have slowly returned from the dead. I almost gave up on you.' She stroked the pink flowers she had nudged back to life when she'd first arrived and pulled at the thorny weeds that were trying to poke their way out of the bed. She moved on to the daffodils that seemed to be wilting and dug around the roots with the trowel she had left at the edge of the bed. They would make it, they just needed a little more love.

It would soon be time to begin the gazebo, the area she had been trying to circumvent since she first entered it. She'd even avoided turning her head in the direction when she worked on the garden bed a few metres away. The thought of it made her shudder and sent tingles down her back. But she knew she was being silly. Just because she had raised herself on her toes didn't mean she wanted to dance again. Just because she dreamed about a dashing man who could lead her around a dance floor didn't mean she was going to pick up her ballet shoes again. A dream? But a dream in which she danced? Did she dance? She still didn't know, but the way her thighs and shins ached, and if the blisters on the back of her feet were anything to go by, she'd guess she did. But what had possessed her?

She had been thinking of her parents more and more lately, always looked skyward, a little smile curving her lips as she did. Perhaps it was the garden, perhaps it was because she felt a sense of home, perhaps because she felt free, and perhaps it was because she had danced. She still missed them so much, even after more than fifteen years had gone by. Her mother's music, the old-fashioned songs that rang out on the CD player, making her break out in a dance when a song she loved came on. She'd pull Alex out of whatever she was doing and swing her around, and Alex would try to copy her mother's feet as they moved quickly across the floor.

Alex knew she wanted to be a dancer from as far back as she could remember, and her parents encouraged her dream, already planning her college applications, VCA, the college of the arts, prestigious and terribly difficult to enter. Her father, a university professor, made enquiries about what she would need, but of course it came down to talent and sheer hard work. And Alex loved to dance so much, she didn't find the hours a day of practice taxing, even though her feet bled and her body ached. Now, after the accident that took her parents' lives, she knew it was never meant to be. She hadn't stepped on a dance floor again.

Now, she shook out of her mind everything that

happened afterwards. She tried not to think about it, what was the point? She was happy here, content, sure, a little lonely, but she had more than she could hope for. Well, at least until December.

A light breeze hit her shoulder and Alex turned around, goosebumps forming on her arms.

CHAPTER 9

It was very early, dawn was breaking through the dark clouds, and her arms were covered in goosebumps. Alex opened her eyes slowly and shut them again quickly. She was disoriented and remained still, listening to her own breathing, loud against the early morning calls of the sparrows, and she willed herself not to freak out. This was all too familiar. The boards beneath her were hard and she slowly reached out a hand that was buried in her chest, feeling the cold wood that surrounded her.

Her eyes flew open and in a second, she was on her feet, jerking her head from side to side, searching for him.

'Where are you?' she cried, spinning around. She moved to the edge of the gazebo and called again. 'Edward, where are you?'

The chirping of the birds was the only response, and a clatter of shaking leaves as a bunch of pigeons flew from their nest, disturbed by her call. She looked skyward and back to the centre of the gazebo where she could now see Edward, his hand on her waist. He twirled her around and the image faded. Alex blinked hard, and opening her eyes, all that was before her was the far side of the structure. She was very alone.

'Edward?' she called, a little softer now. 'Come back.'

A cool breeze blew by and she shivered, looking down at herself, still dressed in yesterday's clothes: jeans, a light shirt and slip-on shoes. She looked around again and shook her head, blinking hard as she did, willing him to return. He didn't.

Slumping back to the floor, she rested her head on the surface, its cold relieving her now hot cheeks. Bringing her knees to her chin, she wrapped her arms around them and a tear rolled off her cheek. It was like déjà vu, but she could picture him more clearly. She could feel her teeth chatter, but stayed on the floor, trying to remember the man who she had danced with again last night, the light-blue eyes that smiled warmly at her and his hand steadying her when she tripped as she stepped onto the floor of the gazebo, but it wasn't a gazebo anymore, it was a dance hall with a polished floor; shimmering light reflected from where she didn't know or care.

She had taken his hand without a thought and let him lead her to the centre of the hall. He held out his other arm and she placed her fingers curved in them, her eyes never leaving his calm ones. Then he gently led her around the floor, and there was music, a soft ballad from a long time ago, a tune she knew but couldn't place.

She squeezed her eyes even tighter, trying to remember the tune now, but it evaded her and the image of him floated out of her head. She tried to bring it back but couldn't. She thumped the floor with her fist and cried his name out again in desperation, knowing it was of no use.

Lifting herself off the floor with effort, a feeling of despair ran through her body and she looked around again. The sun was fast rising, and she looked at her watch. It was nearly six thirty in the morning. With one more scan around the semi-darkened gazebo, she turned on her heel and ran all the way back to the house.

'Where have you been so early?' asked Milly, looking up in surprise as Alex burst through the kitchen door.

'I've been, er ...'

'You've been out all night?' asked Milly, who stopped beating the eggs in her bowl and looked Alex up and down. 'What's wrong with you, child?' Then her eyes narrowed, a little twinkle in them. 'Or more like, what have you been up to?' She put her hand on her hip.

'Nothing,' Alex stammered. 'I just have to change and shower and go to work.' She knew nothing she said was going to make sense to the woman.

'Are you hungry?' Milly called after her.

Alex stopped. She suddenly felt the emptiness of her belly. She hadn't eaten since yesterday morning and the aroma of Milly's baking made her mouth water. She turned back to Milly and nodded sheepishly.

Milly rolled her eyes and continued whirling the eggs. 'Okay, go on, have your shower first.'

Alex turned to leave but had a sudden thought and turned back. 'Hey, Milly?'

Milly looked up from her bowl.

'Do you know anyone called Edward?'

Milly screwed up her mouth and raised her eyes in thought. 'No, I don't think so. Why?' She looked at Alex shrewdly. 'Someone bothering you?'

'No, no. I just … nothing.' Alex hurried to her room.

Her feet felt like fire when she removed her shoes and Alex looked at the time. She could squeeze in a quick bath, just to rid the cold off her and to relax her muscles, which were also aching. Stepping into the hot bath, she sunk low in the large, clawed tub and closed her eyes.

'Edward,' she said softly and her mind floated back to him, the feel of his hand on her back, the other in hers, as he swished her around the floor, his brown hair that fell just beneath his neck, swaying behind him. His smile, slight, at first, and then wide, his eyes crinkling as he laughed. She was smiling too, laughing happily, a feeling of freedom taking hold of her mind and body, something she hadn't felt in a long time. And all the while, the music that played, the tune that was familiar, but not familiar.

It was all still hazy and Alex tried to play it back from the moment she stepped into the gazebo, but just bits and pieces floated into her mind, his broad chest, his even teeth, the way he bowed so low as he reached out for her hand. There was the steady rhythm of his movements, so smooth, so trained … She couldn't remember him speaking, but she suddenly realised she knew his name. How did she know unless they had talked to each other? She squeezed her eyes tight, trying to conjure the memory of what had happened, but apart from enjoying the appearance of his face as they moved to the music, there was nothing. She opened her eyes and looked around for her phone to check the time, but realised she had left it in her room. Dragging herself out of the bath into the coldness of the bathroom air, Alex groaned.

****

'It was a nice dream,' she said to herself as she stood in the centre of the gazebo and spun slowly, hoping he would appear. But the sun, low in the sky, but dazzling, showed no sign of the man she was with last night. 'Edward?' she called softly, still hopeful, and then a rush of guilt swept through her as Nicholas's face swept through her brain. She must be losing her mind; it was bound to happen at some stage.

She looked down at her boots and realised she had thrown on odd socks in her rush to get back here; she had almost run back to the gazebo. She had scoffed down her breakfast, Milly tutting at her the whole time, and thanking Milly with a stuffed mouth, bolted back. But when she arrived, all she saw was the cold gazebo and she felt the shudder that was she was accustomed to now. She picked up the handles of the wheelbarrow that she had left behind from yesterday and moved to the outer edge of the gazebo, sitting on the concrete trim. She opened the cup of coffee that Milly had thrust in her hand on her way out of the house and sipped at it. It burned her lips and she dropped the cup, a flash of his face returning to her.

'Stop it!' she said sternly to herself, and stood up, shaking out her legs to loosen her muscles; they were still a little tight. Maybe a quick run would help, but she looked down at her shoes. No, that wouldn't do. She shook her head free of Edward, whoever he was, and picked up the empty coffee cup, looking forlornly at the black liquid that now washed the soil.

It was nearly lunchtime and Alex headed back into the house. She had barely done anything that morning, her mind distracted by the events of last night, and she constantly looked towards the gazebo, where she hoped he may appear again. But try as she may to conjure him up, he never materialised. She was anxious but also a little relieved that he was undoubtedly a figment of her imagination and she wondered why she was suddenly conjuring up ghosts, but then she thought of her parents and how she still let herself believe they were somewhere else rather than completely gone, and shrugged. She needed to take her mind off things and looked at her watch, glad it was nearly time for lunch. Her stomach felt empty, even after the breakfast she had almost choked herself on this morning.

The soil was hard, even with the downpour of rain two days ago, and Alex dug into it with her hoe, moistening it with a spray of the hose. She was about to smooth out the soil in preparation for after she returned from lunch, when a flash of memory came at her from nowhere.

The photograph! The one Cathy had shown her the day after she arrived at the manor.

She dropped the hose, her heart now thumping hard, and dashed back to the house, as quickly as her tired legs would take her. She bolted through the kitchen past a startled Milly, straight through the quiet house to the dining hall, to the photograph. She picked it up and stared into the eyes of Edward, the man she had danced with last night, the same man who had appeared to her when she first arrived. He was real.

Her knees buckled and she felt herself sink to the floor with a thud, a shatter of glass the only thing she heard before she passed out.

CHAPTER 10

'Maybe we should get the doc.' She heard the voice of Milly close to her face.

'I think she's okay,' said Cheryl's unsteady voice.

The room spun as Alex slowly opened her eyes, and stopped, the blur of round Milly and the looming of Cheryl becoming clear. She could feel her hand being patted lightly and smelled the scent of jasmine close.

'She's coming to,' said Milly, whose arm Alex could feel under her back. 'Alex, Alex.'

'I'm okay.' Alex raised herself to a sitting position and looked to the faces before her, wrinkled in concern. The patting stopped, Cheryl retrieving her hand back. 'What happened?'

'Don't know,' said Milly, still kneeling and supporting Alex's back. 'You ran through the house like a mad dog. What's wrong? Are you hurt? Can you breathe?'

'Yes, I'm fine,' said Alex, looking about her. Little shards of glass were pushed into a pile carelessly, a dish cloth sitting beside it. 'The picture,' she said, looking around for it.

'This one?' asked Cheryl, and kneeling on the floor beside her, showed her the face of Edward. 'What about it?'

'Who is this?' Alex croaked, taking the photograph from Cheryl's hands.

'Why, it's Edward Johns, Rory's granduncle.' She screwed up her eyes in confusion. 'What about him?'

'Is he here?' she asked, knowing it didn't make any sense. Rory's granduncle would have been old, and dead, probably decades ago.

Milly and Cheryl looked at each other and reached out to help Alex to her feet. She sat on one of the dining chairs, the photograph still in her hand, and suddenly realised she was still in her overalls, probably leaving a mess on the pristine green velvet.

'Sorry,' she said, jumping up, and Cheryl gently eased her back.

'That's the least of our concerns,' she said, placing herself on the chair beside Alex and gesturing for Milly to pick up the mess. It was more of a command to leave and she waited until a sour Milly went to the broom closet, came back, picked up the shattered glass and walked out of the room without another word.

Alex was trying to piece it all together as she stared down at the smile she recognised. She knew it was Edward she had danced with last night, but how could it be? She knew it was a dream, but there he was, a real person, albeit dead, in a photograph in the house.

'Tell me, what's going on?' Cheryl poured a glass of water and motioned to take the picture from Alex. Alex pulled back her hand, holding it tight.

'I don't know. I don't know what happened.' She shook her head miserably. What was wrong with her? 'I have to go back to work.'

'Nonsense, not today,' said Cheryl. 'You need to rest.' She paused. 'Milly said you were out all night. Does that have something to do with all this?' This was the most normal Cheryl had been and Alex marvelled how she could take charge when she needed to. 'Maybe you're overtired from whatever … I know it's none of my business, but did something happen to you?'

Alex nodded forlornly and looked up at the concerned grey eyes of Cheryl whose eyebrows were raised, urging her to say something.

'I think I fell asleep out there yesterday.'

'Out where?' Cheryl looked in the direction of the back of the house. 'In the garden?' She looked incredulous.

Alex nodded.

'Out in the freezing cold?'

Alex nodded again.

'What on earth?' She cleared her throat. 'No wonder you are ill. Go and have a bath immediately and tuck yourself up. I'll bring you your dinner.' She tutted and Alex felt like a little child, but soaked it in.

'I still have some work to do,' said Alex. All she wanted to do was go back to the garden to see if he would appear again, to tell him she knew who he was, even though she really knew nothing.

'I'll have none of that,' said Cheryl sternly and tried to pry the picture from Alex's hands. She stopped. 'What's the meaning of the photograph?'

'Nothing,' said Alex and handed it to her, a feeling of loss enveloping her.

Clearly sensing her hesitation, Cheryl pushed it back into her hands. 'If it means that much, hang on to it until we get a new frame.'

'Who is he, really?' Alex asked. She wanted to know

what it all meant, why she saw him, talked to him, danced with him.

Cheryl shrugged. 'He's got a story. I don't know what really, but this was his place. I mean, he built it all. That's why Rory keeps the picture here. Some sort of tribute.' She glanced out of the window and Alex's eyes followed her gaze. Through a gap in a hedge, she could see the gazebo and the hairs on her arms stood on end. 'You'd best ask Rory. He'd know the history of this place, of Edward Johns.'

Making sure she got Alex to her room and asking a number of times if she was okay, a worried-looking Cheryl left Alex with the picture. Alex felt a touch of guilt. The woman had enough on her plate already without her adding to it. She looked down at the face of Edward and pondered the picture. Maybe it had just stayed with her and something about it had conjured him up in her mind, something about his smile, his stance, so straight, clearly in a dance ensemble, brought back things she had long buried. Maybe she was just lonely. But she had danced with him and had somehow spent the night in the cold air. How long had he been with her before she fell asleep? Maybe she was just delirious.

She sighed and followed Cheryl's orders, heading into the bathroom. As she lay there, the hot water soaking through her aching bones, she thought about him again, the picture sitting on the edge of the bath, balanced by a folded towel. He seemed so real, had felt so real, the black sleeves with the white cuffs on which round silver cufflinks sat, she saw as he held her hand in a waltz pose. The scent of soap as he swung her around the floor. The intensity of his eyes against the ruddy face, at odds with each other.

A wonderful dream. Perhaps she had missed dancing and something was trying to tell her that. But she'd always shunned the idea, whenever she felt the urge, whenever she heard the music playing in the background of the Hortitech sales room, a room she didn't like to enter because of it. A fleeting thought of Nicholas hit her and she frowned and pushed him out of her head. Maybe this was her subconscious telling her she should do what she'd always needed to do—dance, another thought she dismissed. But she had danced and it had felt wonderful.

Or maybe it was just a picture she had seen and brought it to life.

'Edward!' She suddenly sat up. How had she known his name? She had never been told the name of the man in the picture until Cheryl had told her afterwards. Cathy had just said it was her grandfather, which he wasn't anyway, but that wasn't the point. She felt a shiver through the hot bath water and the sight of the gravestone she had seen earlier rushed to her mind.

She had talked to him, she must have. She closed her

eyes to remember what he had said, what she had said, but nothing came to mind. She could see his mouth move, but she couldn't hear anything. She collapsed back in the bath with a splash and squeezed her eyes shut. She was overthinking it. Even his face in her mind was blurring, the image that she focused on so avidly disappearing out of sight. It had happened with her parents too. At least she had photographs of them to weep over, to remember clearly every part of them, from their faces to their feet. She opened her eyes again. For now, she had a picture of Edward too. At least until Cheryl reclaimed it.

Hi Mum and Pa,

I don't know what's happening to me. I danced yesterday, so much my feet are swollen and my limbs ache, and with a man who doesn't exist. His name is Edward, and he is so—she held her pen to her mouth, she didn't quite know how to put it—*dashing. Weird, old word, I know, but I can't think of another word. Anyway, I danced. And it felt glorious. I'm sorry. I wish I hadn't, but I didn't even think. I didn't know what I was doing until I was doing it and then I couldn't stop. And Edward was just such a wonderful partner. It sounds so silly, like a stupid dream, and maybe it was. Maybe I was just out there dancing by myself. What a sight, if someone saw me. But no one goes into the garden after dark anyway. I don't know what to think anymore. I knew there was something about that place. I should have stayed away. But I want to see him again. I wish he came back.*

Love and miss you.

The garden looked peaceful in the afternoon sun, the gazebo, far in the distance, a lonely edifice calling to her. She sighed and drew the curtains. Picking up her book, she tried to concentrate on the words in front of her, but they blurred with her thoughts and with her eyes that kept closing. She slept.

A jolt of fear roused her and she sat bolt upright in bed, sweat dripping from her face, and she could feel her nightdress sticking to her back, wet and cold. She gathered the covers around her and held them tightly to her chest, recalling the dream that woke her. The images she had held at bay for so long were back. Her father's face, bloody and already still, her mother's trying to smile at her through the gash near her eye. Her hand being squeezed tightly by her mother's grip, which loosened slowly and finally let go. The feeling of numbness she felt at the time, the same as she felt now, the surreal feeling, not knowing if she was crying, no feeling. Then a sharp scream.

She scrambled off the bed and rushed to the window, searching for the gazebo in the dark, but she couldn't see it, as much as she focused. It was usually there, a beacon that called to her, and now it was not. Throwing on her track pants and her thickest jacket—she was going to be prepared this time—she made her way through the quiet, dark house; the only light

116

leading her was from the glimpses of the moon that sprinkled on the floor in front of her. Creeping through the back door, she tried to run, but the wind of the night slowed her down and by the time she reached its step, she was breathless.

'Edward,' she called.

The only thing that could be heard was the wind and a rustle in the tree above.

'Edward, where are you?' she cried. 'Edward!'

She dropped to the floor and wrapped her arms around her legs and sobbed. 'Edward.' She rocked back and forth, trying to invoke the memory of him again, hoping it would bring him to her, but thoughts of her dead parents pushed into her brain and all that she could hear were the ravaged cries coming from herself.

Shivering, she stood up, and walked slowly back to the house. It was a dream after all.

July 14

Mum and Pa,

Yes, so I think that I've finally lost it. I'm seeing things that are not possible, imagining things that can't be. With you guys, at least I knew what I was doing, somewhere in my mind; I knew you were, well, you know …

But what do I do with this one? He gets into my head when I don't want him to. He isn't real, for goodness' sake! She bit the end of her pen in thought. *Do you think I've invented him so he's easy to let go of, so that I know he's already gone? Ugh, I'm analysing again. I hate that. Anyway, other news, same old, around here. Can't get through to Cheryl, I don't think anyone can, but she's lovely. I know that she's more my age, but I think you, Ma, would have really liked her, would have been friends with her and would have gotten her out of her shell, something which I can't do. I wish I were more like you, like either of you, but I'm a weird one, even I know that. But I think I'm happy here. I love the girls. I don't have the strength to talk about Netty right now, but Cathy is gorgeous. A little sad, a little alone, a little like me, I guess.*

Love you both xx

CHAPTER 11

'Who the hell are you to make this decision?' Rory was yelling. It wasn't often Alex heard his voice raised and she started.

'Half owner,' retorted the heated voice of Samuel.

Alex stopped on the bottom step and stood behind the wall, not wanting to interrupt this exchange, feeling like an interloper. She started to back up the stairs when she heard her name mentioned.

'I thought Alex would be done a lot sooner,' continued Samuel. 'Isn't she a professional?'

Alex frowned.

'Do you see her work every day? She's out there when it's long dark.' Rory defending her. 'If you were in such a hurry, maybe you should have hired more people.'

'Well, it's been three months. I thought she would be

nearly done by now.'

'You hired her in an ongoing position.' Rory's voice was tight. 'At least, that's what you told me.'

'Yes, well …'

Alex retreated up the stairs, and bumped into Cheryl, who looked like she'd been standing there for a while, her hands on her hips, her eyes narrowed.

'Come on,' said Cheryl, moving past her, motioning her to follow.

They got to where Rory sat, his head low and shaking from side to side, and Alex looked up to see Samuel staring out of the window, his hands clasped behind his very straight back.

'What's going on?' Cheryl asked Rory and Samuel turned around, his brow knitted.

'Nothing,' said Samuel and strode out of the room. They heard the front door slam.

Rory looked at Cheryl and smiled wanly. 'Nothing really,' he said; his voice held a note of defeat. He turned to Alex. 'How's the garden doing?'

'It's good …' she started and looked out of the window at Samuel who was already at his car. 'At least, I think it is.' She wanted to ask about her position here. She would need to make a plan if the situation were to change; Melbourne was out of the question for now. 'I've gotten to the inner edge. There's still plenty to plant, but they haven't brought in the order. I think it's going to be held up for a couple of weeks.' She paused. 'Is there a hurry?'

'No.' Rory shook his head. 'No. And from what I've seen, it's looking great. I haven't seen colour in those hedges for … well, I don't remember seeing them look that way, even when …'

Alex was curious. 'Who looked after it all before I got here?'

'We had the local guy come in once a month, just to tidy up. And, well, that's all he did really.' Rory shrugged.

'I've still got some trimming to do,' Alex said and headed for the door.

Rory and Cheryl nodded to her and Alex left.

'Cher,' she heard Rory say behind her.

'Not now, Rory.' Cheryl's voice always changed around her husband as it did now; it became strained, curt, careful.

'Come with me to the stables.' There was a pleading edge in his voice, not a begging, just a tone of desperation, and Alex dropped her head in disappointment. She'd heard many of these conversations before and Cheryl never budged.

'I can't. Netty's having one of those days. I can't …'

'Milly can help out …'

'I said no, Rory.' Her voice shook and Alex walked quickly out of earshot.

It was always this way when the two of them said anything to each other and Alex felt sorry for Rory, who seemed to be trying so hard to connect with his distant wife. She could see him trying to please Cheryl; at times, he'd come behind her and put his arms around her waist, but his efforts were always rebuffed. Alex wondered about them, if this was how it always had been, but she had a feeling that there was once an immense love and there still could be. She was no expert in that, certainly had held herself back from feelings she knew would hurt her eventually, but she wondered about Rory and Cheryl and found herself wishing they could find themselves again. Of course, it was none of her business.

Alex drove the cart around the gazebo and slowed to a stop beside it. She tilted her head and squinted her eyes, trying to see something that wasn't there. Her stomach fluttered and she blinked hard, trying to make him materialise with her will. He didn't and she drove on, banishing the dream from her mind, irritated with herself for wishing a dead man alive. How very morbid. But he wouldn't be the first. She still sometimes believed her parents were alive, wrote to them as if they were, envisioned them living in a place like this not too far away, a place she could go to when she wanted, to see them when she wanted, to talk to them …

She switched her thoughts back to Rory and Cheryl, people who were real; at least, she hoped they were not part of her imagination too. She giggled at that and then frowned, really speculating her sanity. She took a deep breath; maybe she was going mad. But there was Netty, someone who was right in the middle of it all, someone who was between life and death. Netty, who she knew was part of the problem between Cheryl and Rory, not that it could ever be her fault.

Alex placed her bottom on the brick edging of the rose garden and looked back at the sky, little clouds of white floating together beneath a darkening sky. It seemed ominous, a sign of something, perhaps a message from her mother. She looked back to the house in the distance and saw Rory, little more than a speck, heading to his car. She could see the speck pause and turn to the house, his head raised. Then he got into his car and the little Mazda drove away. Again, a sliver of sadness for him ran through her. She may be busy with work and reading and her own crazy thoughts, but she observed much, and knew it had to do with Netty. Cheryl very rarely left the house, most of her time was spent wandering around aimlessly or up in Netty's room. She suspected that the strong-willed girl banished her mother from her space often, for if it were up to Cheryl, she would probably camp out in her daughter's room day and night.

Rory also spent time with his eldest daughter, but he ambled about after he returned from work and Alex could see he was waiting for something to happen, some attempt from Cheryl to show him love or affection, something to show him he still existed in her life. Alex saw him leave some mornings, a suit and tie, somewhat haphazardly thrown on, always with a forlorn glance to the window on the first floor. And most evenings, after dinner was eaten in silence, he'd head to the stables and take his horse out for a ride, even on weekends, after he had spent most of the day with his younger daughter. And Cathy, well, the child just went wherever she felt wanted. Time with her father, time with Milly and time with Alex, but very rarely did Alex see her with her mother and her heart broke for this lost child who was put on hold until the inevitable happened.

Netty. Alex didn't know whether to smile or cry when she thought of the young lady upstairs just waiting for her time to come to an end. But she was elated when one afternoon she looked up from her spot near the azaleas, a movement on the second floor catching her eye. Netty, sitting up in her bed, a frail arm moving frantically to attract Alex's attention. Alex waved back, pleased. She would visit her tonight. It had been a few mind-blowing days and Alex hadn't had the time or the strength to visit her. Cheryl probably needed a break and Alex felt guilty that she hadn't thought about her. She had been going every few days to check on her, to talk with her, to watch a movie together, or just to sit and read magazines in each other's company.

'I won't get to be your age,' said Netty one Sunday when Cheryl had gone to town. Alex had been reading aloud an article on the effects of ageing and what it was doing to the skin of celebrities. She'd scrunched up the skin on her forehead and laughed and Netty had done the same. Then the girl's eyes grew big and she looked away.

'I'm sorry,' said Alex.

'Well, it's not your fault,' said Netty and gave a sad little laugh.

'I still am sorry.'

'Do you know what's wrong with me?'

'Yeah, I think so.'

'I won't live to see my next birthday,' said the girl and Alex felt a stab through her chest. Netty gave a mighty cough and Alex grabbed at the tissue box for which Netty was reaching and turned away when she saw the tissue come away from Netty's mouth tainted with blood. As if sensing Alex's distress, she leaned forward with some effort and laid a hand on her shoulder. 'It's okay. Mum is honest with me about it all. I demand that.'

Alex admired her strength and her maturity. She wondered if that was really how she felt though. She couldn't imagine living every day thinking that it could be your last. Then again, was death out of the blue any better? A fleeting thought of her mother's reassuring eyes the moment before she faded away flashed though her mind.

'Alex?'

She took a breath. 'Honestly, I don't know what to say,' said Alex.

Netty broke out in giggles. 'Yes, that's honest. Most people aren't, not even the doc, who tries to make it sound so … I don't know …' She searched for the right word. 'Hopeful,' she said, then grew serious. 'But I'm glad I got to meet you before I die.'

Alex thought it was a pretty morbid conversation, but Netty had a right to talk about her own death. 'Me too,' said Alex.

'Mum finds it hard to talk about it,' she confided. 'And if I do, she gets so sad.'

'What about your dad?'

'Dad's okay. He tries to be strong, but I sometimes hear him cry. When he sleeps in my room.' She gestured to the spare bed that was always made.

'Well, you can talk to me about it anytime,' said Alex, not feeling as confident as she was trying to sound.

And Netty did. When Alex sat with her on Sundays, Netty discussed the ins and outs of her treatment, her irritation with the doctors and nurses that came twice a week. She talked of her fear of death at times and at others, she'd smile and tell Alex that she was ready. Alex never knew how to respond, but she knew Netty didn't want her to. She just wanted to talk to someone. Her little sister was a source of entertainment for her, coming home from school and discussing her day, performing skits and songs in an effort to entertain her, and Netty enjoyed the nattering of the five-year-old. And Netty talked about her parents, reminiscing about the times they used to love each other, when she was younger and there was hope that she would get better. Now an expression of sadness washed across her face when she talked about them.

'I think they will be okay when I'm gone,' she said one day. "I heard the doc say by the end of the year.'

CHAPTER 12

'How is it all going?' asked Samuel one afternoon, when Alex was heading back into the house. She stiffened when she saw him approach. She really didn't care for the man at all and tried to avoid going into the house when she saw his black Audi parked at the front. He was distant and rigid, but she found him leering on more than one occasion, catching her off guard when she was deep into her work. He'd always look away in what he thought was good time, but Alex was not stupid enough to think he was staring into the fronds with which she was working, rather than at her legs. She may not be the most social person in the world, but she knew when someone was checking her out. Then he'd quickly look away as though surveying her work.

'Good, I think.' She straightened and faced him.

'Hmmm.' He circled slowly.

'It's a lot for one person,' she said hurriedly, and not wanting to sound like she was complaining, quickly added, 'but

I've got most the beds done.'

'What about those hedges?' he asked pointing to the slabs of plants that doubled as fences.

'I was thinking that maybe we could curve the edges …'

'No. I don't care what you do to them. They just look untidy.' He frowned.

Alex wondered if the man smiled at all. 'I was hoping to finish the main rebuilding of the beds first.'

He looked around. 'Yes, well, do you think you will be done soon?'

Alex wondered again about his timeline. 'Is there a timeframe?'

'I said December.' His tone was clipped and he clearly didn't like to waste his words.

'Yes, I think it will be done by then, but the upkeep …'

'That's fine,' he said and left Alex staring after him in confusion. She resolved to ask Rory about it, she'd put it off for long enough. But lately she hadn't seen much of Rory, he wasn't around very much and when he was, he was holed up in his room or in Netty's. She heard them sometimes laughing together as they watched a movie together and she longed for the closeness she used to have with her own parents.

Cheryl still wandered about the place, sometimes approaching Alex in that scared way, trying to make conversation with her, and Alex felt an immense sorrow for her, but she didn't know how to bring her out of her shell, apart from offering her bits of conversation about the garden or commenting on the antics of Cathy, to which Cheryl smiled wanly. She could see the woman wanted to talk more, but she didn't seem to know how, and Alex was no great conversationist herself.

It was a relief not to have to converse with random people, who at times thought it their business to ask about hers. From friendly women in the aisles at Hortitech, who enquired about her life, general small talk that wouldn't make most people uncomfortable, to the leering men who she could see were looking for excuses to talk to her and who would ask her inane questions about gardening appliances which she could see were just pretexts. She preferred being here in the middle of nearly nowhere, where her companions were the flora she cared for with a passion, and the little family whose presence was beginning to take root in her heart.

She was very much on her own right now and had been since she was sixteen; she never counted the two years she spent with her aunt and uncle and chose to never look back on that time with anything, not hate and certainly not love. But there was Nicholas. Those years, as much as she wanted to remember, to ponder, to cherish, she couldn't. Nicholas, the only man she could get close to, the one she trusted, the one she had to leave. She always banished the thought of him, as she did now; there would be no looking back, no going back. She was someone new, a chameleon, who would adapt to her surroundings.

****

It was a warm evening, the moisture in the air unusual for July, and Alex lifted her head to the sky. A flash of her mother's smile shined down at her and Alex dropped to her knees, every muscle in her body letting her down. She wrapped her arms around her knees and let the feeling envelop her. Then she got to her feet and turned to the gazebo, the moon behind it like a halo, and her eyes widened. An incandescent glow surrounded it, even in the light that shimmered through the hedges, and Alex let out a breath. She stood, almost as if in a trance, and peeling off her gardening gloves, let them drop onto the grass beside her. She took a step forward, her heart pounding.

'How are you coping here?'

Alex jumped backwards, completely thrown by Rory's smiling voice. Her eyes left the gazebo, which was now standing dark, a sorrowful structure in front of the darkening sky. Her heart fell and she turned around to look at Rory, whose hands shielded the low setting sun from his eyes, and still donning his riding gear.

She cleared her throat, trying to recover, trying to behave as she would normally, and trying to figure out just what normal was supposed to look like. 'Have you been out?' A stupid question. She retrieved her gloves from the ground behind her and stretched. Her back hurt almost constantly and she twisted around to squeeze her aching muscles.

'Going out, actually,' he said, looking in the direction of the shed.

'It's getting dark soon,' she said, following his gaze.

'I like the dusk, it's peaceful.'

'Anyway, I'm doing fine … I think,' she said. 'Samuel checked it out yesterday.'

Rory smirked. 'Yes, well. Don't taking anything he says to heart.'

'He didn't say much really.'

'Yes, that's what I meant.' His eyes creased. 'He's … he's hard to explain …' He looked at her again. 'What are you doing out here so late anyway? You should have been done for today.'

'I was just finishing the daffodils,' she replied, looking at the yellow flowers that she was still hoping would surprise her. 'It's not that much later. I wanted to start the next bed tomorrow.'

'Well, maybe we haven't said much, but I can already see you're doing a terrific job.' He glanced around him and Alex wondered if he actually noticed that anything was different. 'Are you going to begin working the beds around the grand gazebo tomorrow?'

Alex looked at the darkened structure again and felt a shiver. 'I think so,' she said. She knew she had to approach it at some stage. May as well get to it and defeat the fear that had held her at bay. 'Hey, Rory, can I ask you a question?'

'Anything,' he said and crossed his arms in expectation.

'Is there, er ...' Alex wondered how to put it. 'What's happening in December?'

His eyes clouded and he turned to look at the house. 'Sam wants to sell this place.' He cleared his throat and looked back at Alex. 'I don't.'

'Okay,' said Alex, waiting for something more, something about her job, but asking about it sounded selfish when it was probably the last thing the family would be thinking of.

'I'm fighting him,' he said gently. 'If we stay, if he agrees to hold on to it, we can work something out.'

Alex nodded, still unsure of what that would mean.

'Do you spend every evening out there?'

Alex didn't know how to reply and looked towards the gazebo.

'It's okay if you do. I just don't know how you don't freeze in this weather,' he said. 'Besides, I may have to put a light in the gazebo if you spend so much time in there.'

'I'm pretty rugged up,' she said, pulling at the little fluffy ball atop her beanie. So he'd noticed the times she had been in there, begging for Edward to return. She determined right then to stop going to that ridiculous place.

'I can see,' he said. 'Anyway, just don't go getting sick.' He began to walk in the direction of the front of the house and stopped, his brow knotted. 'Why do you go all the way around the house?' he asked.

'Because that's the way in?'

'But it's further away.'

She didn't want to tell him it was Samuel's instruction to her when she'd first arrived. Besides, it was a quieter way into the house, and she generally went unnoticed on her way in and out.

'I prefer the walk,' she said, and he raised his eyebrows, clearly not convinced.

'I'd better be off,' he said and started away. He turned around. 'Are you happy here?'

That was unexpected and Alex wasn't sure how to answer. 'Yes.' That was the right response.

Rory twisted his lips in a smile that suggested he didn't believe her. 'Better get in soon. It's already dark.' And off he strode towards the shed.

Alex packed her golf cart and looked back at the gazebo. It stood majestic against the pink of the sky and seemed to beckon to her again, the glow around it expanding before her eyes. She ran back to the house as quickly as her feet could take her.

She returned to her room, which was now warmer with the little portable heater that Cheryl had bought for her. She thought about what Rory had asked. Was she happy? She felt contentment, she knew that, a peace that she hadn't felt for a long time, but happiness? She could barely remember what that felt like. But now a sliver of fear struck her.

In a matter of months, she may be asked to look elsewhere for work and then what? She would have to leave this place. At that moment she knew she didn't want to. She wanted to stay in this little nook of the world forever. She could probably find a place near town and travel to work, wherever that would be ... It was a beautiful little town, which she was getting quite used to now, travelling back and forth a couple of times a month when the need for supplies grew urgent.

Samuel may help her find something, or even know of someone who needed a landscaper. He had been around several times in the last month, more often than he did initially, but she still didn't like the man and always tried to avoid him when he was around, escaping to the garden where he sometimes found her, so asking for his help was out of the question, particularly when she had never been in the habit of asking anyone for favours. But she was sure Rory would help her find something, a place, a job. He was clearly well loved in these parts.

But what would become of them if they had to leave? Her concern for them unnerved her. She had remained aloof to most people, unknowing and purposefully detached. But Rory and Cheryl seemed so ... she couldn't think of the right word ... awkward, at least with each other, but they both had taken her as part of the furniture, and when they asked her to treat their home like her own, they clearly meant it. She had never once felt in the way, even when she had inadvertently walked into their stilted conversations with each other. She felt sorrow for these people and a sense of helplessness, feelings that were not common to Alex, who had avoided people for exactly this reason, they would go from her life too. She felt irritated with herself for letting them get to her, for making her feel something more than apathy towards them. She was better off alone, protecting her heart from pain.

Even Milly had grown on her, the always bustling housekeeper, who complained about her husband and talked about her friends, and Alex listened every morning, enjoying hearing about the everyday lives of people whom she had never met and was never likely to. She would miss the woman when it was time to leave.

When these thoughts got to Alex, she went to her garden, lovingly attending to the weeds, talking to the flowers.

'You're a beauty,' she would say to the lilacs, which were her favourites. They seemed to be strong and steady, weathering the conditions under which they were placed well. 'I wish I could stand it all. I wish I had the guts to bloom wherever and whenever.' She'd brush her hands lightly over them, trying to wield some of their strength.

On other days, when her mood was light, she'd look to the chirping birds in the tall trees and call to them, mimicking their sounds. She even made names for them, Fruity and Blossom, Snappy and Poopy, her regulars, who were always out to welcome her into the garden. She sometimes forgot which was which, but she tried to at least get a glimpse of them each day as she travelled to the area in which she was working.

Once every month, the lawnmower man, an older gentleman with grey hair and a creased forehead, came with his ride-on mower and doffed his cap to her as he circled round the grounds. She'd wave at him but he never stopped to make conversation with her, his intent to finish and leave as soon as possible. For him it was a day's work, to her the work was every day. But it was something she felt like she could do forever, despite the solitary nature of the job.

'Are you lonely?' Cheryl asked one evening after she had wandered into the garden, a cup of tea and a tray of biscuits in her hands. She set them down on the handle of the wheelbarrow, which was filled with mulch. Alex had been planting a new batch of azaleas which surrounded a patch of little trees.

Alex shrugged. She'd reflected on this question a lot lately. 'Yes, and no. I have my garden, I have Milly, Netty … and you,' she said, and smiled, embarrassed.

Cheryl planted her bottom on the small wall where Alex sat. 'I know it's none of my business, but …' She fingered the flowers, still in little pots beside the wall. 'Do you have a man … or woman, whatever?'

Alex thought of Nicholas. 'No.'

'You don't go off the grounds a lot, do you?'

'I don't have any need to really,' said Alex. 'I have everything here. I have good food, I don't need many clothes,' she said gesturing to her overalls. 'I even have great entertainment, a library full of books that will take a lifetime to read.'

'Are you on social media?'

'No.' Alex thought of her inactive Facebook account and how she stopped the urge to reactivate it whenever she felt desperate to know what was going on in the world, particularly with Nicholas. But she knew that would lead to trouble she couldn't deal with right now. 'Never really used it much anyway.' She didn't have many friends, real or virtual.

'Me neither.'

They sat in silence, Alex munching on her biscuits, and drinking coffee, trying to keep her red curls from flying into the cup.

Cheryl smiled at her attempts to tuck her hair behind her ears. 'You have great hair,' she said.

'Ha-ha, thanks for being nice. I can't tame this, no matter what I do,' she said, pulling one of the locks and stretching it out. 'It could do with a trim though,' she said, making her mind up to go into town on the weekend.

'I could try?'

Alex looked at Cheryl in surprise.

'I do it for Netty and Cathy.' She screwed up her face. 'Sorry, probably not the clincher.'

'No, I think their hair looks great.' It was not something Alex had particularly thought of before, but she recalled both girls' hair, thick, dark, Netty's always long, flowing to her waist, little waves beside her temples, and Cathy's shorter, with tempered bangs framing the plump cheeks. 'I didn't know you did that. When you have some time, that would be great. Thanks.'

'I'd be happy to,' said Cheryl and rose to leave.

'Did you want to hang around while I work?' Alex could see that Cheryl was feeling like she was in her way.

Cheryl paused for a moment and then looked back to the house. 'Netty,' she said, and Alex nodded.

Alex sat on her haunches, watching Cheryl's departing figure, wondering about her. She determined to make more of an effort with her. The woman was obviously more lonely than she was, if she sought her out for company.

'I'm not the best company,' she said to herself and got back to work.

****

She walked through the path to the golf cart and was glad it was the end of the day. Netty and Rory and Cheryl were on her mind, Cheryl running out of the house this morning, Rory chasing after her. She could see Netty's parents were unhappy and lonely. She knew what loneliness was, but it was part of her life. It was the only thing she knew how to be. Even Nicholas couldn't fill the holes that engulfed her. Nicholas … 'I will love you forever.' She heard his words echo through her brain and she pushed him from her mind again.

It was the end of July and bitterly cold, but Alex would not use that as an excuse for not working as she usually did. Besides, as much as she shivered through the day, she loved her work. Each bulb she planted, she treated with love, each dead plant she removed, she did so with sadness. But she knew this was not going to last. Her time here had an end point, if Samuel got his way.

She glanced at the gazebo as she walked by. It didn't scare her now. It had been weeks since she had seen the apparition, which she knew now was part of her imagination, her lonely, vivid imagination. The shivers she had gotten when she got close to it before had also gone, along with her hope that Edward would return. Those first few weeks, after that night, she had been back every evening, calling for him and waiting until the late hours of the evening until she was too cold to stay outside. She didn't really understand why she wanted him to come back, as it had scared her so; perhaps, she thought, it was evidence that she was not going mad. Milly was long gone by the time Alex returned to the house each evening, her heart sad, her hope vanishing. Each night she vowed she wouldn't return, and each night she did. But he never came back.

CHAPTER 13

'Cry if you need to.' Alex held Netty's hand, and the girl frowned at her, a deep cavernous wrinkle between her eyes.

'No!'

'It's okay,' said Alex.

'It's not okay,' said Netty, her eyes brimming with tears.

'Tell me what happened, all of it.'

Netty folded her arms and turned her head away. Alex wanted to smile at this, knowing how maturely Netty usually tried to behave. The doctor had just left and the news couldn't have been very good. It was a Sunday, not his usual day, so something was off.

'Okay, well, if you don't want to talk about it, I guess we can just watch a movie or something.'

Netty nodded and Alex skimmed the programs on

Netflix.

'That one,' she said, when Alex scrolled past *Dirty Dancing*, and Alex's heart skipped a beat. She hadn't watched that since … it was her mother's favourite.

'Is that too adult for you?'

Netty rolled her eyes. 'If I'm not going to get to be an adult, then so what?' she said. 'Besides, I've seen it many times. It just makes me happy.'

'Okay.' Alex clicked on the movie and felt shivers run through her body before the music in the opening credits even began and her eyes blurred, but she couldn't leave Netty in the state she was in. She'd seen Cheryl run out of the room in tears, bumping into Alex in the hallway, and Alex had rushed in to find out what was going on. She found Netty tearing up a piece of paper, the remains of which were now strewn on the floor beside her bed. Alex had not attempted to pick them up, knowing that it was the cause of the problem and not wanting to interfere. She busied her mind with all things gardening while Netty stared at the television.

'Do you know my dad and mum used to dance together?'

'Oh?'

'It's in the family,' said Netty. 'Dad's family were dancers

144

a long way back.'

Alex's thoughts flew to Edward whom she hadn't tried to think about anymore.

'I wish I could dance,' she said. 'Do you like to dance, Alex?'

'You can always dance in your head,' said Alex. 'And no. I don't dance anymore.'

'Anymore? Why not?'

'Well,' she said, taking a deep breath. 'There's no one to dance with.'

'You don't have a boyfriend?'

Alex shook her head. 'And I don't want one either. I'm happy by myself.'

'Yes, yes. I know. You and your garden.' She rolled her eyes.

Alex nodded and continued to watch the moves her mother and father would do so easily, the image of them replacing that of the characters on the screen.

'I don't have a lot of time left,' said Netty softly.

Alex jerked her head in her direction, shocked. 'What?'

'Doc said to Mum it was soon. Almost everything is not working anymore.'

'Bugger what the doctor says. You look good today.'

'I try to, Alex, but it's hard. I've been sick for as long as I've been, well, alive. They've tried everything, even though they know it's no good.' She let the tears roll down her face now. 'And I try too. I try for Mum, but sometimes I can't be strong for her. She has to be strong for me.' She lifted her frail hand to Alex, who took it, giving it a squeeze.

Alex nodded. 'You don't have to be strong all the time.'

'I know.' She looked back at the television and they both stared at the vision of bodies pressed together, moving sensually to the music.

'Will you miss me?'

Alex felt her throat tighten; she had been trying to hold back the tears herself. Someone had to be strong. She nodded.

'I'll miss you too. Wherever I am,' said Netty simply.

Alex watched until the end of the movie, enthralled and sad, and when it was finished she looked to Netty, who was asleep, her head leaning against her pillow. She just looked like any normal teenager who had fallen asleep in front of the television, not one that was fighting for life. She left the television on and went out of the room, her heart breaking for the little girl who lay so peacefully on the bed. She passed Cheryl, who was sitting on the settee in the parlour, her head resting on the back, her eyes closed. She shook her shoulder lightly.

'Alex,' said Cheryl when she opened her eyes. 'Is she …?'

'She's asleep now.'

'I don't know what to do, Alex,' said Cheryl, and ran her fingers along her temples. 'She's not got long. What will I do?'

'Well, for now, let's get a cup of tea.' Alex offered her hand and Cheryl gratefully took it.

****

The night was warmer than usual for August and Alex threw on her long puffer jacket. Sundays were meant to be her day off, but she sometimes worked through, even if it was just moving about the grounds to survey its needs. Today she'd stayed in, trying to avoid the cold, but now after her time with Netty and the news she'd been given, Alex sought the peace she needed. She'd let Cheryl cry as she told her of the few months at the most Netty would have left. After more than an hour, Cheryl

147

realised the time and had run off to check on her daughter. And Alex had sat alone in the parlour, feeling shell-shocked.

Her heart was breaking for them, Netty and her mother, and she was acutely reminded of her own parents, the film they had watched not helping matters at all. She wished she had brought a cup of coffee with her, something to keep her warm, but she didn't want to turn back. It was already past seven; the moon was high and she didn't want to bump into Rory, who had taken Cathy out for the evening. She hoped they had returned by now.

She walked to the gazebo tonight; she hadn't been there since she worked on the planter boxes that surrounded it, some days ago, but she found herself drawn today, and allowed herself to be carried to it, her heart heavy. She entered and sat on the wooden seat along the edge, and she let herself cry—for Netty, for the girl's parents, for her own and for herself, something she'd stopped doing some time ago, a complete waste of time. Long howls she let loose, as she hugged herself, her knees tucked into her chest.

'Alexandra.'

She opened her eyes, her head still buried between her knees, and sniffed.

Silence.

She kept her head down and sobbed softly, wiping the moisture from her chin.

'Alexandra.'

She froze for a moment and felt a hand on her knee. She wasn't afraid. She lifted her head and looked into his eyes.

CHAPTER 14

He stood before her, straight and tall, the tails of his tux falling to his knees, his head bent to her, as his shoulders remained straight. One hand was held behind his back and the other he now put forward, palm up.

Alex blinked hard and on opening her eyes, still saw him there, just a hint of a smile on his lips, a glint in his eyes. She squeezed her eyes shut again, willing him to be there, a small part of her wishing he wasn't.

'Edward.'

'Alexandra,' he said again and her belly swilled at the sound of his voice.

She lifted her lids and saw the hand nearer to her. She reached for it and rose to her feet, his hand guiding her towards him.

'Dance with me,' he said.

Alex tucked her hand over his and put the other on his arm just below his shoulder, her eyes looking up into his soft blue eyes that were deep set under hooded eyebrows. She could now feel his hand on the back of her waist gently nudge her forward and she felt herself move. It seemed like the most natural thing to do, move around the floor with this stranger, her steps closely following each one that he took.

Before she realised it, a song was playing slowly, the same one she remembered that had played before: Mozart, she recognised now; not something that she'd listened to often, but part of her music selection for her dances. She gazed at him and he stared back; all that she could feel was the beating of her heart as she moved to the rhythm. It was the waltz, a dance she had rarely performed as it had never been her favourite, but whether it was her or this dream, she did it with ease, her back erect, her feet moving as though they were made to move this way. She tilted her head to the left, and felt herself being swept to one side, the violins making her stomach catch, their melancholy tune sweeping her up in their plight.

And then it was over. He twirled her outward and she was left holding on to his hand, which she gripped tight, afraid to let go, should he disappear altogether. Facing him, she put one foot behind the other and curtsied, the same time as his shoulders bent forward in the smallest of movements.

'Hello, Edward,' she said, still clutching his palm.

He smiled broadly and led her to the edge of the gazebo and looked into the garden. Alex followed his gaze, the moon now clear in the sky, lighting the wisps of the grass that shifted with the breeze. She turned to look at his profile as he smiled with satisfaction, his head moving slowly to survey the garden.

'You've done a splendid job,' he said, facing her, his smile widening. 'A wonderful thing.'

'Who are you?' Alex said in wonder. 'What are you?'

'I'm Edward.'

'I know that much,' she replied, still staring at him, fearing if she turned from him, he would vanish. 'Why are you here?'

'I'm here,' he returned. 'Why are you?'

'For you,' she said, not shy or afraid as she felt she should be.

'You came back. I waited.'

Her eyes creased. 'I came back every day. I called you but you didn't come.'

'I didn't hear you,' he said. 'Come, let's dance.'

Alex looked back into the gazebo. 'There's no music.'

'You don't hear it?'

And she could; another waltz played around her, the music coming from nowhere, and she was in his arms again, moving more quickly in this music, her body finding the rhythm easily, her feet moving in step with his. She felt alive, like she was born to dance with this man who smelled like soap, who moved like silk. Around the gazebo they went, covering the whole floor, and Alex was flushed when the music stopped and Edward let go of her hands as she tried again to hold on to his.

He bowed again and looked up at her with a twinkle in his eyes. 'Shall we do it again?'

Alex shook her head this time and then stopped, worried that he would leave her again. 'Will you disappear?'

'Why would I do that?' His voice was teasing, his eyes small slits.

'Because you did the last time.'

'Come with me,' he said and she followed him to the railing. He turned around, leaning on the post and crossed his arms casually. 'I see you every day. I watch you in the garden.'

'Then why didn't you come back?'

He looked steadily at her. 'How did you feel after I came to you the first time?'

Alex shook her head in confusion. 'I don't know …

terrified, confused ...'

He nodded. 'I couldn't do that to you again.'

'Then why did you come back today?'

He took her hands. 'You needed me to.'

She felt the strong fingers curve around hers and felt a jolt through her body. 'Edward.'

'You've said my name a number of times.' His voice was deep, soft and had a formality she rarely heard.

'I'm sorry,' she said and laughed nervously. 'How old are you, Edward?'

'That's an audacious question,' he said, raising his brows, and he leaned his back on the railing, putting a thumb in his pocket. Alex felt her knees weaken. He looked like a tuxedo-clad James Dean.

'Sorry,' she said. 'But if it helps, I'll tell you my age.' She smiled mischievously and was unnerved by her forwardness. She was flirting!

'A little minx you are,' he said and grinned. 'Well, I'm forty-one.'

'You look ...' She caught herself. She was indeed being audacious, something she was not usually, at least in her real life.

'I look …?' He cocked his head to one side.

'So, tell me, Edward, what's with the dancing?'

He was standing before her in a second. 'Would you like to do a round again?'

Alex wanted to laugh. He sounded like something from an old movie. 'No, I want to talk to you. I want you to talk to me. And I want to remember everything you say.'

'Oh?'

'I didn't the last time. I didn't remember anything.'

'That's because we didn't speak, not very much.' His eyes glinted and Alex was suddenly wary.

'What did we do?'

'Why, we danced, of course.' His eyes widened in shock at her suggestion. 'My dear Alexandra, whatever were you thinking?'

'I don't know,' she replied, embarrassed. 'But I found myself on the floor asleep in the morning without much of a memory of what happened.'

'But you knew it was me,' he said and smiled. 'You came back for me.'

Alex reached out and touched his arm, feeling for the

realness of her dream, something she could think of in real terms when the memory tried to escape her again. Edward glanced at her hand and put his hand over it, and Alex felt the heat course through her.

'You dance very well,' he said, clearing his throat and removing his hand.

Alex shook her head. 'I haven't danced in over fifteen years.'

'That won't do,' he said and moved towards the middle of the floor and Alex heard the music magically begin again. 'We have some making up to do.'

Glad he didn't try to enquire any further, she smiled and put her hand out to him.

CHAPTER 15

Her alarm went off and she stuck out her hand to click the snooze button but realised it was time to get up. She groaned, her body aching, and her eyes suddenly bolted open. Jumping out of bed, she dashed to the bathroom, had the quickest shower of her life and back in her room, looked over the hedge at the gazebo, so far away. For the first time in months, she stopped to survey herself in the mirror, quickly throwing on a sliver of mascara and a dash of lip gloss, even attempting to tame her wild hair with a pin. She mussed it, pulled it this way and that, and shrugged, resigned to its unruliness. She sprinted down the stairs, where she was stopped in her tracks by the raised voice of Cheryl coming from the dining room, which she had to go through to get to the kitchen.

'… and what were you thinking?'

'I was thinking that we are going to fall apart,' said Rory's voice, subdued, sad.

She heard Cheryl sigh and waited at the bottom step, feeling like an intruder on this conversation between husband and wife. She wanted to go back up the stairs but she was keen to get to the gazebo, where she hoped Edward was waiting for her as he promised. But to enter the room would be worse. As she deliberated her next move, she heard Rory again.

'We are still here too.'

'Not all of us will be soon.' She heard Cheryl's voice crack and Alex's heart skipped a beat.

Silence.

Alex tiptoed back up the stairs and moved back down, thumping loudly on the wooden boards, alerting them to her presence. She couldn't stay on the step forever and she couldn't go back to her room, she had to get to work. Besides, she felt like an interruption would be welcome and even necessary. She plastered on a smile and came into view of Rory, who stood by the window looking outward, his head resting on his arm, and Cheryl, seated at the dining table, her head in her hands, her shoulders straightening at the racket Alex had made.

'Good morning,' chirped Alex, sounding cheerier than she felt. Her elated mood had collapsed at the brief snippet of conversation she'd just caught.

'Good morning,' mumbled Rory, looking at her and

trying to smile through his crumpled face. Cheryl didn't look at Alex but mumbled something, looking towards Rory as he walked out of the room.

'Are you okay?' asked Alex, unsure of what to do next.

'Yes.' Cheryl raised herself from her seat, looking as though it required great effort, and walking past Alex, she patted her on her arm before continuing away, up the stairs.

Alex let herself down on the chair Cheryl had vacated and felt a deep sympathy for these two people who were in so much pain. She wished she could help them somehow, and looked back up the stairs, contemplating peeking in on Netty, but she would be resting; she never woke this early, or at least that's what she'd said.

She sighed and as she looked up, she saw his face, back in a new frame, placed on the table near the window. She had reluctantly returned the photo after taking a picture of it with her phone. She knew every inch of his face now, from the large forehead to the bottom of his clefted chin. A sense of excitement ran through her again but with it also came a twinge of guilt. She felt it was almost morbid to feel happy when other people in this very house were suffering.

She went, more slowly now, to the kitchen, which was empty, and she wondered where Milly was. A plate of scones with butter and cream sat on the bench with her name on a little torn piece of paper, and Alex smiled appreciatively at the thoughtful woman. She poured herself a cup of coffee and let her mind wander, allowing herself to let the previous night sink in, while she nibbled on the scones, marvelling at Milly's cooking skills, something she never fully gained herself.

She contemplated her evening with Edward. Yes, of course he wasn't a real ghost. It was something she'd conjured up. An apparition to comfort her, because she couldn't give any part of herself to a real person. Nicholas flashed through her mind and as usual, she banished the thought of him. There was no space for him in her life anymore.

Edward had smiled when she asked if he would be there the next day. 'Yes, if you would like,' he said with a little bow.

'But you weren't before,' said Alex, worried that he would disappear once again and not return.

'Alexandra, please trust me.' He let his hand slide down the side of her face, and she felt an electricity, feeling it again now as she sat at the bench, and she stroked her cheek, trying to recapture the sensation. She gobbled two scones, swallowed down her coffee and raced towards the shed from where she needed to collect her seedlings.

Piling all she needed for the day into the golf cart, she sped to the gazebo, wishing she was working near it today. Instead, the seedlings needed to be planted a hundred metres away around the cupid statue, and she'd put it off for too long already. Nevertheless, she took a detour past the gazebo, and stopped in front of it. She stepped out and looked at the structure. A chill went through her. Maybe he wouldn't be here today. Maybe it was just random, his appearances. She headed in. She couldn't control it, whatever happened.

'Hello, Alexandra,' he said from somewhere behind her and she jumped.

'Edward,' she replied, relief flooding her body, her knees weakening. 'You're here.'

'I did tell you I would be.' He beamed and she had to stop from throwing herself into his arms.

'I have to work there today,' she said, pointing in Cupid's direction. 'So I can't stay in here long.'

'May I join you?'

She looked at him dumbfounded. 'You can leave this place?'

He laughed lightly. 'Of course I can. I can go anywhere, at least around the grounds.'

'I thought you were … I don't know … trapped in the gazebo?'

'No, my dear. Would you mind if I accompanied you?'

'Yes ... I mean, no, I don't mind,' she said, and wondered if she did mind. He would see her in unholy positions, digging and pulling out weeds, her hands full of dirt, sometimes even her face streaked with it. Then she remembered that he told her he had already seen her working and she wondered how close he had come to her before. It certainly explained the shivers.

She went back to the golf cart and looked at him in confusion when he didn't get in. She unloaded two buckets, one with her tools and one with grass seeds.

'I'm terribly sorry I can't help you with that,' he said, a crease in his brow as he watched her wheel the barrow forward.

'So tell me.' She was curious. 'What are the rules?'

'The rules?'

'You know, the rules. Like, what you can and can't do.'

'Well,' he said and stopped walking. 'I ... I don't really know.'

She dropped the handles and touched his arm. 'You have worn the same outfit the two times I've seen you ... well, now the third.' She chortled. 'Don't you change?' she said, a glint in her eye.

'You're teasing me,' he said. 'Yes, so I see.' He looked

162

down at his dress and put his arms forward to survey them.

'How long have you been here?' She picked up the barrow again and kept moving, her eyes still on his face, which now bore a slightly confused expression. The way he walked, his back so straight, one arm behind it, yet a saunter, made him so attractive, and Alex was surprised at her thoughts. She'd never been so attracted to someone before, save for Nicholas, but with him it had been more than just attraction. Could she fall for Edward like she did with Nicholas? Even if he wasn't real?

'I don't know.' He put his forefinger to his chin and looked thoughtful.

'Do you see other people?' She took a breath, wondering if she had finally gone completely mad, asking strange things of a dead man.

'I see you. I see Rory and Cheryl ...'

'You see them too?' Alex wondered why she felt disappointed. 'Do they see you?' she ventured, wishing they didn't.

'No.'

A thud of satisfaction hit her heart and involuntarily, she smiled.

'Does that make you happy?'

Her face flushed. 'Hmm,' she said and kept walking, while he walked silently beside her.

'Did I tell you how lovely you look today?' Alex didn't risk looking at him, but she could feel her cheeks redden, glad she had taken the extra few minutes to tame her hair. Absently she tucked a curl behind her ear.

'Thanks,' she mumbled, glad they were at the Cupid statue. 'Here we are.' She faced him now. 'And now, what will you do while I work?'

'I will keep you company,' he said. 'I wish I could help.'

'How is it you can touch me, I can touch you, but you can't touch anything else?'

'I don't know the "rules", as you say, Alexandra,' he replied and his eyes widened in horror. 'Are you proposing I am shirking work?'

Alex was taken aback. 'Oh no! Oh gosh, no!' She was horrified he thought she was suggesting that. 'I was just trying to figure it all out.' She reached for his arm.

'Yes, you can touch me,' he said and put his hand on her chin. 'I can touch you too.' He leaned closer and Alex felt his breath on her cheek, which he now let slide against his lips. 'And I can kiss you,' he whispered.

Alex closed her eyes and felt her knees buckle, reaching out for his arm to steady her.

'Alex.'

She opened her eyes to see Cheryl walking towards her and looked around in panic. Edward was not there, and she was bent forward awkwardly, one hand on Cupid's knee.

CHAPTER 16

'Are you okay?'

She saw Cheryl hurry over and straightened herself, feeling dazed. Cheryl was beside her in a second, her hand on Alex's elbow, her scrutinising face in front of Alex. Alex nodded and looked around again. Edward was gone.

'I brought your coffee,' said Cheryl, offering Alex her travel mug that she'd left on the kitchen counter. 'You must have forgotten it.'

'You didn't have to,' said Alex, really wishing Cheryl hadn't. It made Edward disappear. 'But thank you.' She took the mug and sipped the coffee, which burned her tongue.

Cheryl giggled and then stopped in horror at her action. A tear welled in her already red eyes.

'It's okay to laugh sometimes,' Alex said, reaching her hand out to Cheryl's, who let her take it.

'I have to start,' said Alex, gesturing to the garden bed.

'Oh, I'm sorry,' said Cheryl and made to leave.

'But I have time,' continued Alex, noticing the distress on Cheryl's face. 'Let's just enjoy the sun that doesn't show up too much these days.' She looked up to see a cloud part, the dawn having broken not even an hour earlier.

'It's beautiful, isn't it?' Cheryl gazed at the sky and surveyed the garden. 'Do you love what you do?'

'Yes, I think so,' said Alex.

'I can see why.' Cheryl smiled and then her brow knitted. 'Can I ask a favour?'

Alex nodded.

'Can I help you out sometimes? You know, when Netty is resting?'

Alex didn't know how to reply. This was her employer, she had no business helping the help.

'Sorry, am I impinging on your space?'

'No, of course not.' Alex waved her hand about, understanding the woman was lonely. 'I don't know if you will want to.' She hoped that would put Cheryl off, but then she saw the sad look on Cheryl's face again. 'But you're welcome to try for as long as you want.'

Cheryl looked down at her clothes, her black skirt and white blouse, tied at the throat with a sash. On her feet were black leather shoes with a little pointed heel. Alex always wondered why she dressed herself up every day when she went nowhere. 'Maybe not right now though.' She laughed, and again straightened her face almost immediately. 'But thanks,' she said and wandered away.

Alex took a sip of her coffee again, still feeling the sting of the first burn on her tongue. 'Hey, Cheryl,' she called and Cheryl turned around. 'Thanks,' she said, lifting her mug.

When Cheryl was out of sight she looked around, hoping Edward would materialise again. But as she worked throughout the day, in a minor state of panic, he didn't come to her. She examined her work at lunchtime and was disappointed with herself. The roots of some of the magnolias were showing through the soil, which was clustered in uneven mounds. Her head was not in it, nor was her heart today. But her stomach was growling, so after another glance around, she headed back to the kitchen.

After a quick lunch and a chat with Milly about the lawnmower man not arriving until next week, she returned to her place in the garden to fix the mess she'd made in the morning. She was behind schedule now. She was hoping to cover the garden with water and food as she usually did in the afternoons, and looked up at the cloudy sky, wishing for rain. Even though she'd given up hope that Edward would return today, she gazed at the gazebo, a lonely figure in the mist.

At four thirty, the end of her day, she trudged back to the main house, satisfied with the work she'd done, yet disappointed she'd not seen Edward again. She had glanced at the structure so many times during the day that she found her neck in pain, more so than usual. Stretching her muscles, she twisted and turned before she entered the kitchen.

'You look a sight,' exclaimed Milly, who was garnishing a salad. The smell of a roast nearly done wafted into Alex's nostrils and she inhaled audibly.

'Long day,' replied Alex. 'Something smells good.' She took another deep breath.

'Nearly ready.' Milly gestured to the inner door, which Alex was heading towards. She needed a bath before she had dinner. 'Just watch out in there. Mr Samuel is not in a good mood.'

Alex rolled her eyes. 'Thanks, Milly.' She really wasn't in the mood to be lectured on the timeframe of the garden again. She hoped she could sneak by unnoticed.

She heard Samuel's raised voice as she took the stairs

and was tempted to pause to hear what the issue was today. It was always something with him. He was either yelling about the place being half his or lecturing his brother on his choice of career. Rory, a teacher at the high school in Chernut, seemed to enjoy his work, but his brother, a lawyer in Melbourne, was always telling him how he was trained as well as him.

'You can do so much more,' Samuel was saying.

Alex sighed. It was the latter today. She resented Samuel for making Rory feel like a failure, Rory, who was probably more successful at his job, doing what he loved, and being loved for what he did. Yet he was made to feel less than by a snob of a brother, who thought he was more successful because he was a lawyer.

'Sam, give it up, will you?'

'I can't understand you. We had everything the same. In fact, you got more, and you waste your time …'

'I love what I do,' said Rory.

'But how far will that get you? You would be able to buy me out …'

Alex could feel her chest tighten, unable to listen to more. It was none of her business anyway, not this. She managed to get away without being seen and before she headed into the bathroom, glanced out of the window, watching the silhouette of the gazebo through the darkening sky. It seemed so forlorn, so lonely, and she had the sudden urge to run back to it. She didn't, she couldn't lose her mind even more, but as she curled up in the bath, thoughts of Edward returned. Returned really wasn't the word; she had thought about him all day, but now she could really savour the thought and shivered in the warm bath as she felt his lips on her cheek, his soft voice tickle her ear. She closed her eyes and lay her head back on the towel. She didn't need to banish the thought of him. He was safe.

After checking in on Netty, who was asleep, Alex went back to the kitchen. An hour had passed and her food was served and placed on the kitchen bench. She ate slowly, her head beginning to bow from the weight of sleep. She wandered back to her room, settling for an early night, perhaps a bit of reading. Getting into her pyjamas, she turned on her little heater and folded down her bed. The empty space in the other side, the place Nicolas would have lain, saddened her. The image of Nicholas, a book in one hand, the other holding the blanket aside for her to hop in, flashed through her mind and the sliver of sadness she felt, she quickly brushed away again. She went to the window as she did every night and looked out to the gazebo.

Through the dark, cloudy night, she saw a glow, almost like a halo surrounding it, and her eyes widened and her heart skipped a beat. Throwing on her dressing gown, she headed back out the door, her heart thumping loudly. She needed to get to it before it was gone or he may not appear again. She just couldn't tell when he'd be there and when he wouldn't, but she was going to find him tonight.

Flying past an astonished Cheryl going up the stairs, Alex didn't even pause to acknowledge her. She dashed out the back door with all the speed she could muster, her aching limbs and neck forgotten. When she got to within sight of the structure, she could see his silhouette in the middle of the doorway and tears began to fall with sheer relief. She kept running, her dressing gown flying behind her, her bare feet not feeling the grass and mud she trod through.

The world spun as she fell into his embrace, her lips on his, the salt of her tears on her tongue. He picked her up off her feet and she was weightless, a feeling of nothingness surrounding her, a feeling of something so strong, so all consuming, nothing she ever remembered feeling before. Then she was back on the floor, her eyes searching his astonished ones, and she moved back to the safety of his arms.

'Don't leave me again,' she whispered.

August 21

This has turned out to be a strange job. I say that in the best way and maybe the worst. There's so much going on right now I don't know where to start. So maybe I'll begin with Netty. I don't want to think about what's going to happen and I almost wish I wasn't here to see it. I know now that I'll probably be leaving come December, that man isn't going to let up, but I think it would be better if I weren't here when she goes, you know? That way the family can grieve by themselves. They don't need me around, they won't want someone around who's not family anyway. She held up her pen and breathed deeply. Who was she fooling? She had always been honest with them even when they were alive. *I guess I'm being a coward. It's easier to say goodbye to someone who is alive. I know that's for sure.* She thought about Nicholas again. She wasn't so sure. *Either way, I don't think I have any say in it all anyway. Other news—Cheryl and Rory are still the same, but she's opened up to me a lot. Not sure how I feel about it, but I really like her, not just because she seems lonely, like me, but because I can see she is such a good person, kind, generous and we just seem to click. I've never had that before, not a real friend.*

Okay, the good news. He came back!!! I'm still worried he won't, not always, but gosh, he is swoonworthy! I'm a crazy wreck when he's with me, and even when he's not. My nerves seem to be shot all the time; it can't be good for my heart. He walked with me, he was such a gentleman, and my gosh, he can dance. He could give you a run for your money, Pa. She swallowed. *Yes, I danced with him again. And yes, I enjoyed it. I'm sorry. I don't know what I should do but I want to. It was so natural and I felt like it was back then when everything was so good, before everything happened. I hope I see him tomorrow, and the day after that.*

Goodnight, love you.

CHAPTER 17

'I want to,' said Cheryl, her overcast eyes looking towards the house. 'But I can't talk to him anymore.'

'You at least have to try. He loves you. It's plain to see.' Alex followed her gaze.

'I don't know anymore.'

Alex didn't want to interfere in anyone's business, but she felt a pang of sorrow every time she saw either of them, their broken hearts written all over their faces. She decided to change the subject.

Cheryl had become a regular companion to Alex, even buying herself dungarees and a checked shirt, looking very suspiciously like the one Alex wore often. Cheryl had donned a pair of brown boots, laced up to the middle of her shin, and had flowered orange-and-white gardening gloves. When she had first come out, a couple of days after Alex had invited her to, Alex wanted to smile at her enthusiasm, but the anxious eyes of

Cheryl stopped her.

She didn't do very much but helped Alex with retrieving implements from the wheelbarrow or golf cart, things that Alex was quite capable of doing herself, and at times her slowness was a bit of a hindrance to the pace of Alex's work, but she knew Cheryl wanted to feel like she was helping. At first it bothered Alex, as Edward would always disappear whenever she arrived, but now, three weeks later, she knew Edward was always going to be there and she knew he was around even when Cheryl was, sometimes sharing little smiles and laughs with him. And when dusk set upon the garden, she was all his, no one in the house questioning or even noticing when Alex sneaked out every evening.

Now here was Cheryl, obviously in love with her husband from whom she felt so distant. She saw Rory look at her as she floated by, pain and longing in his eyes. She wondered where he rode off to each night and hoped that it wasn't as ominous as she thought. Cheryl barely left the grounds and when she did, her trips were brief; even her visits to Alex in the garden were short, her eyes darting to the manor often. She didn't want to leave Netty alone, it was obvious, but she found some pleasure in the company of another person, and Alex could tell she was beginning to consider her a friend.

Cheryl didn't have many friends, as Alex had suspected, her life being taken over with caring for Netty from the moment she was born, and Alex wondered if she had any family near or far, someone who she could vent to, someone who could understand what she was going through. She worried that Cheryl would become dependent on her friendship, and for that matter Alex worried that she was doing the same. It could be taken out of both their hands.

'Cathy was born from a moment of passion, of absolute desperation,' she admitted one afternoon. Her eyes teared up and Alex felt a little uncomfortable. No one except for Nicholas had opened up to her before. She was just never the sort, always kept people at arm's length and loneliness was what she chose. She wasn't going to feel sorry for herself, but it kept her heart safe. 'I don't do justice with that girl. But Rory takes her out often. Especially now that she's started school. She makes friends easily.' She stopped. 'And I feel terrible because I know she'll be okay. She's tough, one less thing to worry about.'

'Cathy is a great kid,' Alex said, not quite knowing how to respond.

'She is,' Cheryl replied, a sad smile shadowing her face. 'And I'll have more time after …' This time the tears fell and Alex, as awkward as she felt about it, moved closer to Cheryl and let her weep on her chest.

Cheryl talked non-stop now, about Netty, about Milly and how long she had been with them, about her own family who had disowned her for marrying Rory, who as much as he had a name, was not good enough for the likes of the good folk of Toorak.

'We met at a club,' she had said, laughing. 'When he lived in Melbourne in his university days. Of all things, a club.' She shook her head, passing Alex the bucket of mulch, which shook her hand from its weight.

'That's as good a place as any,' replied Alex, taking the bucket before Cheryl dropped it.

'But it wasn't a good match for them, my parents.' She was not smiling anymore. 'But no one was good enough for their princess, even a man with a massive house like this. Even his name, one of the oldest in Melbourne.'

'You can't please everyone, I guess,' said Alex, remembering Aunt Helen, whose face came before her now, the woman she pretended didn't exist since she walked out of her home more than ten years ago.

'What about you, Alex?' said Cheryl. 'You are this mysterious creature who no one has any inkling of.'

'What do you mean?' Alex laughed nervously. She didn't think she was a great mystery; she didn't think anyone even noticed her around, much less think about her.

Cheryl looked at her with creased eyes. 'Never mind.'

Alex didn't want to pursue this line of conversation anymore and tried to change the subject. 'So, what about Samuel? What's his story?'

'Samuel is just worried about money. It's always money with him. His wife is much the same. We don't really see much of them unless it has to do with the house.'

'Is he … not …' Alex didn't know how to put it.

Cheryl laughed mirthlessly. 'Oh, he's well loaded. His problem is …'

Alex could see Cheryl didn't really want to talk about Samuel anymore.

As if reading her mind, Cheryl waved her hand about. 'I don't want to talk about Samuel.'

'Okay,' said Alex, and she took a breath. 'What do you know of the owner of this place?'

'Who? Samuel and Rory own the house.' Cheryl looked at her, confused.

'No.' Alex laughed. 'I knew that much. I meant his ancestors, the ones who built it, or began this, or …' she muttered, not really knowing how to mention Edward by name.

'Oh, you mean the Johns?'

Alex nodded.

'They made their money in wheat, not far from here. Then they bought all this land, built this house and there isn't much more to it. No skeletons, pretty squeaky clean, really.'

'Who was Edward?' Alex blurted. As much as she saw Edward, there were things she felt she couldn't ask.

Cheryl smiled and nodded. 'Oh, now we get to it. The photograph. What was with that?'

Alex felt her cheeks grow warm. 'Nothing. Just reminded me of someone, that's all.'

'Who?'

'Edward,' she said, shaking her head. 'Tell me about him.'

'I don't know much. Like I said, not many skeletons, but something strange about him. He was Rory's great grandfather's uncle. Died in the 1940s, I think. He built this place. I know he was a great dancer. There are pictures of him at the town hall.'

Alex was curious and tried to pick Cheryl's brain some more, but Cheryl had no more information to give. And why would she be interested in some distant relative of Rory's who died so long ago, when she had so much more to think about?

'I have to go back,' said Cheryl, looking at the gerberas

179

that lined the other end of the gazebo. 'Will you be okay with those? That gazebo gives me the chills, I don't know why.'

'Yes, I should be fine. I'll finish them up and do the watering.'

'Oh, I love the watering! I'm going to try to come later tomorrow, so I can do that with you.'

'That would be great,' said Alex, trying to sound encouraging. She loved watering with Edward, where he would put his arm around her as they walked through the garden, sometimes in the freezing cold. But at least there was today.

When Cheryl had gone she turned to the gazebo and saw him materialise. She was used to it by now, but her heart always skipped a beat, a tingle in her belly always present.

'A lonely lady,' observed Edward.

'Yes, she is,' said Alex, recognising a lot of herself in her new friend. 'But a strength she doesn't know she has and one she's going to need.'

Edward looked thoughtful.

'Are you okay?' She laughed. 'Of course you're okay.'

'Does the gazebo give you the chills too?' A teasing smile played on his lips.

'Well, to be honest, yes, it used to. But now I look forward to them.'

He looked down at her and knelt to level his eyes with her. 'Will you leave?'

Alex was taken aback. 'What do you mean?'

'Are you going to leave here?'

Alex shivered. 'I don't know. I hope I don't.'

The days were getting longer already and Alex was reminded that December, whatever that held, would be upon them in a few months.

August 31

Hi Mum and Pa,

Edward. I think I'm falling in love with him. I yearn to see him every moment he's not with me. When he is, there is no one else in the world. And yet, I know he is transient. I want to ask him more about it but I don't want to drive him away again. And I'm scared too. I can become attached. I already am attached. Then what's going to happen in December? That's coming up, a few months, I know, but what then? I shouldn't think about it. I want to enjoy him without being afraid. But I am afraid. And then there's the family. They are real. Them I will miss. I'm already getting too close. I don't want to but I feel like they need me. Maybe I need them. Sorry, this ranting is so nuts, but I thought you should know what I'm dealing with, maybe send a sign? Look at it this way, at least I have something to tell you now.

Love you more than ever. xx

CHAPTER 18

Samuel was on the back porch when Alex came in after her day; a long, tiring day trudging through mud that felt like clay was done. Under her boots, thick mulch elevated her by two inches and she needed to take them off before entering Milly's pristine kitchen. Milly would not be impressed if she left a mess on her polished floor and Alex didn't want to give the woman more work than necessary. She sat on the porch step and took off her boots, thumping out the mud from them on the garden bed beside her. The mud was already hardening and she dug into the treads trying to wrench it out. It was going to be a taxing job. She groaned. All she wanted to do was have a quick bite to eat, shower and return to Edward, who would be waiting for her. She just left his side but if it were up to her, she would live there, but she needed to survive. As it was, she was thinner than usual, her jeans hanging off her, held up with a belt she had to purchase from Chernut. And she needed to bathe and slap something on her face, the streaks of mud on her chin were not becoming.

'Hi, there,' called Samuel and Alex jumped in fright and looked behind her in surprise. He was never cheery, so she was lost for words. 'Good day?' He actually smiled, something she had never seen him do before. It was unnerving.

'Er, yes. I think it's coming along quite well,' she stuttered.

'I noticed,' he replied, his eyes scanning the side of the garden but looking at nothing in particular. 'Sit with me,' he said, gesturing to the chair beside him.

'Okay,' she said, wondering what he needed to talk about, and placed herself on the edge of her seat.

'Are you liking it here?' He swirled the glass of whiskey in his hand.

'Yes, I am,' she said and a smile crept to her lips when she thought of Edward, but suddenly realising who was sitting next to her, she stiffened.

'Don't get too used to it,' said Samuel and sat back in his chair, a strange look in his eyes as he surveyed her, his eyes resting on her chest for a second and then turning away quickly.

Alex nodded and turned to look at her boots, cursing them for delaying her. She felt distinctly uncomfortable, nothing particularly new to her, but she didn't like this man and his slurring didn't help. She wished she could just go inside.

'You know, you are quite pretty,' he said.

Alex glanced up at him and squirmed in her seat. 'Thanks,' she muttered. She never felt she was ever pretty. Her hair was too curly, her eyes too big and her mouth just seemed to take up most of the space on her face, leaving hardly much room for her nose, which seemed to fly off her face. A ski lift, her mother used to tease her when she was little, knowing quite well it was from her who Alex received it. But pretty, no. She never had that illusion. It was weird to hear Samuel say it and a thought of Nicholas flashed through her mind again. She'd been thinking about him far too much lately, odd really since she was so taken with Edward that her former lover should have been far from her mind. He was the only one who ever called her pretty, not even Edward did.

'No, I mean it.' He leaned forward, setting himself on the edge of his seat. 'You are quite attractive.'

'I have to go inside, get changed, you know.' She shifted and began to raise herself.

'Just sit with me for a while,' he said softly, taking her hand, his narrowed eyes boring into hers. She jerked it away in horror, wondering how the earth just turned itself on its head. 'I'm sorry, I didn't mean to scare you. I just thought that … well, whenever I'm here, you don't seem to be and I feel like I haven't gotten to know you at all.'

'There's not much reason to,' said Alex, staring into those ice-blue eyes, surprisingly similar to Edward's. 'I'm your employee. As long as I do what you need me to …'

'But don't you get lonely out here, all by yourself?' He took a swig of his liquor and nodded towards the house. 'All that is here is that. How can you bear it?'

Alex widened her eyes. *That* was his family in there. 'They are good to me. Cheryl is lovely and Rory …'

'Yes, yes,' he replied impatiently. 'But it's all doom and gloom in this house. Don't you want something more?'

'I'm doing okay,' she said, getting up.

Samuel rose at the same time, his face so close to hers she could smell the whiskey and tried not to offend him by cringing. She hated that stink, it brought back too much … She reared back, turning her face from his, but he didn't move and she could feel his breath on her ear.

'I need to go in,' she said, shaking.

'I just …' he said, almost a whisper, and Alex turned and fled into the kitchen.

She slammed the door behind her and raced past an unnerved Milly moving through the dark hallway, a tray in her hands. Slamming the bathroom door shut behind her, without meaning to, she halted, troubled by her reaction and more anxious about what might have happened. She leaned on the sink and looked at her reflection in the mirror. She absently wiped the brown streaks from beneath her chin.

'What just happened?' she whispered to her reflection. 'Did I just imagine that? Did I take it the wrong way?'

She didn't know the answer to either of those questions, but the reflection that stared back at her didn't give her any reason to believe that Samuel would come on to her. Her curls were unruly as usual, her mascara, as thinly as it was applied, was smudged under her eyes, and the big eyes that stared back at her didn't seem to in any way beckon to anyone. She sighed and turned on the bath. She was hoping to have a quick shower, but she needed time to calm down before she returned to Edward.

Edward. Also a figment of her imagination, a beautiful hallucination, for sure, but he wasn't real and would not last forever. Nicholas was real, he could have lasted forever. No, she couldn't risk that. She closed her eyes and Samuel's face came to her, his ogling eyes, his breath. A tear began to fall and she sat up in the bath in anger. Grabbing the loofah, she scrubbed hard at the soot from her face and hands, cleaning not just the dirt she could see but that she could feel, the grime left in her bones from Samuel, her boss. She tried to but couldn't understand what happened. He had leered at her, surely, but he was always treating her like the help, which was fair enough, because she was the help, but why had she suddenly become attractive to him?

It had to have been the whiskey. She knew what that could do, but she also knew by now that that was the weakest excuse made by the weakest men. Right now she was at a weak point too, memories of her life after the accident swimming through her mind, the emergence of Edward bringing back things she preferred not to remember. Her dancing, her utter joy at moving around the gazebo with Edward, what her dancing had done and what came afterwards. Patrick, her uncle, who wouldn't leave her alone, always the stench of whiskey on his breath, and drops of spittle finding their way to her cheeks as he tried to grope her buttocks, the lewd comments when her aunt was not around. And Helen, her aunt, who treated her with disdain, like an orphan, which she was. Her aunt's face swam beneath her eyelids, as Alex sat hunched in the bath, her eyes squeezed shut in anger. Helen's jaw which jutted out in hate, her eyes narrowed to the tiniest slits, but even through the narrow gaps, Alex could feel the hatred that bore through her.

A teenager she was, and now as she thought of them, she hated them even more. They should have been there for her, they were family; she had lost her parents and they were all she had. How she had resented her parents then, for leaving her alone, for not alerting her to the world of evil that lived beyond the safety of the walls of their life. She had to discover it on her own, left alone in a house with two people who despised her presence and treated her like a servant, her own kin who she'd never gotten to know before, reviled by her presence.

Alex fisted her palms tightly and let a low growl escape before shaking off the image of those people. She had to let it go; she thought she had. And she had to decipher what was real and what wasn't. She was surely losing her mind. The thought of losing Edward chilled her and a flutter of fear touched her heart. No, she could live in this fantasy, for as long as she could.

She would just have to steer well clear of Samuel from now on. Besides, she had enough to make her happy, rather than dwell on a man who was as unpredictable as the weather. She paused. Edward had been unpredictable too. She smiled as a warmth flowed through her and then she frowned. Nicholas had never been unpredictable. He had always been there, had never left her side, never let her down.

She went to bed that night confused, thoughts of Edward and Nicholas battling in her brain.

****

'My parents had a garden with a little pond,' she said. They sat on the stone bench that faced a miniature granite waterfall, one of their favourite places to go on their walks. 'Nothing as elaborate as this thing, but it was really cute, a little waterfall that flowed down into the water. My mum loved it.'

'Tell me about them,' said Edward, his head leaning on Alex's which was nuzzled in his neck.

Alex's face glowed. 'I can't describe it, Edward, they were so real and beautiful. I try to remember, but it's also so painful. I hate them sometimes for leaving me.' She was not smiling anymore.

'They didn't deliberately leave you,' he said, tightening the grip on her fingers.

'When I was a kid, I used to hear these awful stories of terrible parents, of children who were treated badly or not noticed by their parents. Friends of mine even. And I couldn't understand it. I would try to sympathise, especially with my friend Paulina, whose parents didn't even know she existed. When she'd come over, she would want to stay and of course my parents would let her, but she'd always want to keep staying over. I thought she was being dramatic, especially when we got older, but I began to see the way her mother was with her and I thought it was odd the way she didn't even acknowledge ...' She looked up at Edward. 'Am I boring you?'

'Why, no.' He planted his lips on her forehead. 'I would like to hear more.'

'I used to dance. I was to go to a college, specifically for performing arts. I was going to be a professional dancer,' she said suddenly, a mischievous smile on her face, and watched as his eyes lit up. In the two months since he'd begun visibly frequenting the garden, Alex wasn't sure she wanted to tell him about her past, especially a past she hadn't thought about in a long time, one she told herself she preferred to forget. Not anymore.

'Alexandra!'

'I'm sorry I never told you before.'

'You have been dancing with me for …' He put his forefinger on his chin and his eyes creased. 'How long has it been, Alexandra?'

It worried her that he lost track of time. She didn't know what it meant, but he never seemed to know how long ago it had been since he first appeared to her.

'Two months,' she said. 'I know. I should have said something, but it's a part of my life I've tried to forget.'

'But why, my love?' He turned her shoulders towards him and Alex discerned a troubled look in his eyes.

'Well.' She shrugged. 'I did it until I was sixteen,' she said, allowing herself to remember the wooden boards on which her pointed toes skipped over lightly. She told him about her life before the accident, about how she lived in a fantasy world before then, and how her life really began on that night. And then she was telling him about Patrick and Helen, her mother's sister, her uncle and aunt, who never really wanted to take her but had to because there was no one else. Her elderly grandmother was in a nursing home and had no means of caring for her as much as she wanted to. But life at her aunt's house was horror and she understood now what her friend Paulina felt— unwanted, even abused verbally. She knew she had to leave. Living on her own, she picked up a job at a nursery and her love for growing things began, or when she allowed herself to remember her own garden, the one she grew up with, with her parents.

'That was where I met Nicholas,' she said, her voice softening.

'Nicholas?'

'I don't want to talk about Nicholas,' she said and closed her eyes tight.

'He is important to you.' It wasn't a question.

'Not anymore,' Alex replied, tears trying to find their way out of her eyelids. She wished she didn't still love him.

'Will you tell me about him one day?'

'One day,' she said and leaned into his arms. 'I don't

want to go back,' she said.

'Go back to where?' His head sprang back to look at her from a distance and Alex felt her heart catch at his worried expression.

'To the house.' She laughed and squinted her eyes at him. 'What did you think I meant?'

'I thought you meant away. From here. From me.'

'I don't want to ever leave, Edward, ever.'

And yet as she put her head on the pillow that night, she wondered how long this was going to last. She was in love with a ghost.

September 12

Dearest Mum and Pa,

I may be finally going mad. I'm in love with him but how do I know? How can I know? He doesn't exist. But I wish he did. I feel safe with him; I feel like I am floating on clouds and this time I can. With Nicholas, I couldn't let myself be happy. Something always held me back and I think I knew I was eventually going to lose him. How could someone put up with a person like me? I couldn't give him all of me. You took most of me away with you. I'm sorry. I don't mean to blame you.

Alex looked at the pile of letters and turned it upside down, gazing at the first few she'd written to her parents, letters of resentment, of despair. She wondered why she kept them, but she knew she needed to know how she felt when she was alone; it wasn't something she wanted to forget. They were there to remind her that whenever she got to be too happy, too content, as she was when she was a sixteen-year-old, it could be taken away in a flash. She fingered the string that tied together the pile and sighed. She turned back to the letter at hand, wondering whether her parents read them, heard her …

But now I wonder how I could have been in love with Nicholas. No, I don't think that … I'm just so confused. Nicholas is real and I think I still love him. He jumps into my mind more than I want him to. Then there's Edward, so real, so not real, and I think I'm in love with him too. You must think I've gone mad. Maybe I have. But there is happiness in this madness, even if it will end.

I love you and I miss you.

CHAPTER 19

'How about that song?' Netty paused the DVD. The Righteous Brothers halted their crooning of 'Unchained Melody' as Alex watched the movie intently, her fingers entwined, her knuckles pale. Netty had suggested watching *Ghost*, and Alex suddenly wanted to see it desperately. She'd heard of the film, of course, but had never seen it before, the story about being in love with a ghost. She wanted to know what would happen, how this would end, how it would end for her and Edward.

'Song?' she asked, woken from her reverie, slightly irritated.

'For my solo.'

Netty had been trying to choose a song, a surprise for her parents, but each time she lifted her voice, she was tired and her tune ended in rasping coughs. Alex tried to humour her, knowing she wouldn't be able to make it through a few lines, let alone a full song, but she let Netty try, encouraging her and slowing her down when she got breathless.

'Oh. A bit slow?'

'Slow is best, don't you think?' She had a wry smile on her face and Alex grinned.

'Yes, probably. It's a good song. I like it.'

'You've heard it before?'

'Yes, a long time ago,' said Alex, the familiar tune from her childhood reaching out to her. But she hadn't listened to music, at least not intentionally, since the accident and avoided it at all costs.

'Do you like music, Alex?'

'I used to …' She paused, thinking of how her home was always filled with song, from music of the sixties to those of the early 2000s. 'I don't listen to music very much now.'

'Why not?'

How could Alex explain to a fourteen-year-old the way her heart hurt when she heard an old tune, even a new one, how she repeated mantras in her brain to drown out a tune, especially one that played in her house, and ones that her parents danced to. How she couldn't listen to the operatic ballet tunes that would set her toes on pointe no matter where she was, and the dashing feeling of guilt when she realised what her body had done in the gazebo, when she spun around and the exhilaration she felt, how it had betrayed her will. And how she welcomed it back now, guiltless and yet not. She shrugged.

'Does it make you sad?'

'I guess so.'

'Can you tell me why?' Netty reached her hand to Alex's shoulder, and she felt a warmth for the girl. Another one she would lose. At least she knew this was coming.

'My parents loved music. I was a dancer.' She smiled when she saw Netty's eyes widen. 'Until I was sixteen.'

'What happened when you were sixteen?'

Alex told her of her performance, how it was exquisite as told to her by her audience after it was finished. She told her about the applause, the 'bravos' called out to her, while she looked into the crowd and found her parents' faces, shining with pride. It was the best night of her life up to the very hour. She knew right then that she was going to make it into the VCA, the Victorian College of the Arts, she explained, when Netty's brows knitted. Netty nodded knowingly and moved her hand to Alex's fingers that were clutching tightly to the edge of the bed.

'So what happened?' Netty was whispering.

Alex turned her palm around and Netty slipped her

hand in it, her eyes still wide and questioning.

'That was the night my parents left me,' she said, thinking about how she always said it that way when people asked. They left her. Abandoned her. They didn't die, they left her alone. She looked at Netty, whose jaw had dropped slightly.

Alex cleared her throat. 'They, um … there was an accident on the way home from the recital. I remember this massive bunch of roses that they got me and I held it on my lap in the back seat. And then, well, I think I forgot some of it, but the car was crashed and they were gone.'

Netty's hands were both now on her mouth. 'Oh Alex! I didn't mean …'

'It was a long time ago. Fifteen years.' Alex managed to keep the tears at bay. 'And I haven't danced since then.'

'What did you do? Where did you live?'

'That's another story for another time,' said Alex, getting up. She needed to breathe and let the water out of her eyes before the dam burst in front of this impressionable young woman. She had enough sadness, she didn't need more. 'You need your rest. I've excited you quite enough for one day.'

'But we haven't finished the movie.'

'We can continue it next time. Or you can go ahead and

I can catch up another time.'

Netty unpaused the movie and Alex went to the door.

'Hey, Alex?'

'Yes, Netty?' said Alex, not wanting to face the girl.

'Do you believe in ghosts?'

Alex smiled. 'Yeah, I think so.'

CHAPTER 20

Alex was heading out for her morning run when she bumped into Samuel, huffing into the back door. She started in surprise. Samuel never came to the house so early and he looked visibly upset. His brows were knotted and his lips were pursed, not unusual for him, but this was different; he looked scared. Alex paused to stare at his retreating figure as he pushed the inner door with such force, it banged against the wall. She wondered what his problem was this time, but she was certainly not going to ask.

She continued on her routine, one she tried to keep up with, feeling like her body was too stiff. 'Dance is the best exercise,' said Edward with a wink, but Alex knew she needed to have a minute to herself and it wouldn't do to let her good habits slide.

It was on the way back as she passed the stream when she heard a galloping behind her and turning around, saw Rory pull up.

'Hey, there,' he called down. 'Need a lift back?'

'Kinda defeats the purpose, doesn't it?' she said, looking down at her track pants.

'I guess so.' He dismounted. 'Mind if I stroll with you for a while?'

'Sure,' she said. She was used to Rory by now, when he stopped in the garden, making conversation with her about Netty and Cathy and constantly asking her if she was happy at Lovelet Manor. She could see he was unhappy when he talked about his wife, even thanking her for letting Cheryl help her with her work.

'Did you speak to Milly, by the way?'

'I haven't seen her since yesterday morning. Why?'

'A man came here asking for you. I asked her to tell you.'

Alex stopped in her tracks. She began to shake and forced herself to focus on the track beneath her feet.

'Are you okay? Alex?' Rory, who had continued to walk and found her not beside him anymore, turned and peered down at her in concern.

Alex nodded. Nicholas. She blinked twice and looked up at Rory, still staring into her face while his stallion shadowed his every move.

'What did he look like?' She found her voice, gurgly, but perceptible. She didn't need a description, who else could it have been?

'He had … I don't know, brown, dark brown, maybe black hair. He was tall, wore a leather jacket.'

In spite of herself Alex wanted to smile. It was a description from a man who really didn't notice details. But she knew it was him.

'He said his name was Nicholas. Do you know him?'

He could have started with that, thought Alex, feeling faint, and she forced one foot in front of the other. 'What did he want? What did you tell him?'

'I didn't tell him anything.' He looked proud. 'He asked for Blanche first, then he asked for you. I thought it was odd, so I preferred you know before I said anything.' Clearly the man was more perceptive than she had given him credit for. 'Should I have let him in?'

'No.' Her response was too quick and she glanced at Rory and began walking again. 'Thank you.'

'Said he would be in Chernut for a couple of days. He left a number.'

She knew the number. She walked with Rory in silence.

'You know you can talk to us about anything. We are like your family. Netty is so fond of you; Cheryl, well, I don't know what Cheryl will do if you leave …' He laughed, a nervous chortle.

Alex was barely listening anymore. She tried to stop the trembling in her fingers and tucked her hands in the pockets of her jacket. How had he found her? Her heart thudded against her chest now. Nicholas. It seemed like years since she had seen him and yet it had only been a few months. She had tried to put him right out of her mind when she got here and wouldn't give herself a chance to think about him, but that hadn't been working as much as she liked. She couldn't think of him. She knew she would be tempted to return to him and she couldn't. And he had clearly not forgotten her either.

'May I have the morning off?' she asked Rory suddenly. She had to see him, to know.

He smiled knowingly. 'Of course. You don't have to ask. Bridgeton Hotel.' He smiled wryly. 'The only hotel in town.'

****

She drove out of the grounds feeling the same nervousness that usually hit her when she left, but now she was shaking. The thermos of coffee beside her was not helping, but she needed something to do. She wished for a moment she smoked. It was nine thirty when she reached town and parked outside Amber's shop. She looked towards the hotel, Bridgeton plastered in dark-brown letters on white stone, and spotted his green van immediately. She waited in her minivan for half an hour and chewed her thumbs, her eyes never leaving the hotel. Her thermos was dry and she considered going into the café to get a fresh cup of coffee, but fear held her glued to her seat. She turned on the radio for the first time since she got the car some years before, and nothing came out of the speakers. She fiddled with it, trying to get a station, but she figured there would only be so many stations in a small town. Nevertheless the fiddling kept her distracted.

A tune came out of the speakers suddenly, one she didn't know, and she was about to continue scrolling through the stations when a movement caught her eye. She looked through the windscreen and saw him. Her heart caught as she watched him open his car door and retrieve something from the glove box. Probably his wallet. He always seemed to leave it lying around. He closed the door of the van and stood looking back at the hotel. He seemed unsure as to what to do next and she watched him, clutching at the steering wheel, her heart telling her to run to him, her head telling her to run the other way. He took a step towards the door, his long legs getting him there in three strides.

'Turn around,' she breathed through gritted teeth. It would take the decision out of her hands. She would have to speak to him if he saw her.

But he didn't. He disappeared into the hotel and Alex turned on the ignition and sped out of Chernut as fast as her minivan would take her.

****

'You're not yourself tonight,' said Edward that evening.

Alex hadn't been herself all day. When she arrived back at the manor after arguing with herself the whole way back, she was mad with herself, angry she had the chance to talk to him and had scurried away like a terrified rat. She almost turned back a number of times, but fear had already taken hold. How would she explain herself? What if he didn't want her anymore? But he was there … for her. But what if he asked her to come back to him? She wasn't sure she wouldn't have said no. And then she'd be back where she started. Back in Melbourne, in a place she now could never think about returning to. No, she couldn't see him; not now. She was still too weak.

After getting into her work clothes, she headed to the garden, keeping a distance from the gazebo. She didn't want to see Edward right now; moreover, she didn't want him to see her in this state. She contemplated her work at the end of the day, unhappy with her progress, even after spending an extra hour in the garden trying to make up for the lost time. The gerberas were looking sloppy, the apple trees she intended to finish pruning were done haphazardly and she would have to fix the damage tomorrow. She hadn't focused on her work, not completing what she'd wanted to, including the mulching, which she left half done. Her mind was cloudy and her stomach in knots. How had he found her? Did she leave a clue somewhere? But no, she hadn't seen him for a week before she left and apart from the scant furniture in her little flat, she had taken everything. She had even forfeited two months of rent in order to get away as quickly as possible. Had she been careless, had Nicholas gone back to the flat and found something? A piece of paper, the advertisement? No, she'd taken it with her; it lay in her suitcase with all the other mementos of her life in Melbourne. And yet her heart beat with a hunger for him.

Edward had appeared to her after lunch when she walked back to the garden and she had been quick and blunt, unable to hold a sustained conversation with him, her mind wandering to Nicholas at every turn. When she began the watering in the afternoon, their favourite activity together, where they just got to chat and laugh and hold each other's hands, he had followed her around in silence for a little while and she hadn't even noticed when he disappeared. When she did realise he was not behind her, she sighed.

'Sorry, Edward,' she said to the air and kept walking, wishing that the sprinklers reached all the way past the garden beds and she didn't have to do them. She was not enjoying this walk today.

In the evening, before she headed out to the gazebo, she took little care of her appearance, which was now unusual for her. Since she began making her nightly visits to the gazebo, she'd put on a sliver of make-up and had even visited Chernut to purchase a few new clothes, mostly dresses, and Edward had noticed the difference. 'You ought to wear dresses more often,' he'd remarked. 'You have the loveliest legs …' He'd caught himself and blushed, but not as brightly as Alex had.

Today she threw on a pair of jeans and a sweater without much thought and her hair was wild and unpinned. And for the first time, she didn't want to go to Edward. She felt guilt-ridden. She was thinking of Nicholas and going out to see the man she thought she loved, she was betraying Edward; yes, an apparition, she reminded herself, but that ghost cared about her too. And Nicholas, whatever would he think if he knew she had left him for a ghost? She looked out of the window into the dark night and almost wished the gazebo wasn't lit up. He was calling her, inviting her to come to him and she had to go.

'Isn't that a beautiful purple moon?' said Edward,

squeezing her hand. They sat together on the step of the gazebo looking over the pond in clear view of the moon.

Alex took a moment to understand what he had said and looked up at the moon, a pale yellow, disappearing behind light clouds. 'What?' She looked into his playful eyes.

'I'm a selfish man. I just wanted your attention,' he said sheepishly.

'I'm sorry,' she replied, wishing she could forget about Nicholas, as she had tried to do for the last few months. Sometimes she had been successful, but today her efforts were in vain.

'Did something happen today?'

'No,' she muttered. 'Yes.'

'Would you like to share whatever it is with me?'

Alex thought about it. No, she didn't want Edward to know about Nicholas. That was her past. Edward was her … What was he, really? 'How long can this go on?' She stood up and looked down at him.

He raised himself and peered intently into her eyes. 'Alexandra?'

'No, Edward. Seriously. Are you going to be gone? When?' She knew she was being unreasonable and he didn't have an answer for her as much as she didn't.

'I … I don't know.' She saw him lose his air of self-assurance for a moment.

'I am alive, Edward. You are not.' She saw him flinch. 'This is not a love story. This is some fantasy I've created to escape reality.'

'My dear Alexandra!' He moved towards her and she shrank away, watching his hands drop limply to his side while the crease between his brow deepened.

'I need to go,' she said, turning from his face which was filled with anguish. 'I need … I don't know what I need.'

'Yes, if you must,' he said, stepping back, and she raised her eyes to watch as he disappeared.

Digging her hands into her pockets, she turned and walked back to the house. As frustrated as she felt, her heart ached for Edward. She knew she'd hurt him and maybe that was her intention. How long could it go on like this? A sudden stab hit her chest. What if he didn't return to her? She turned back to the gazebo, but the glow it had before was now gone. He was gone.

Maybe it was time to leave, maybe it was time to step back into the real world and face what she must. Would he still be in town? Should she face him, try to … No; she pushed the thought from her mind, but lately this technique wasn't working very well anymore. Her mind awhirl, she made her way back to her room.

She heard soft music playing in the living room and she paused on the bottom step. Even though she usually avoided anyone, especially in the evenings, she had the urge to stop and see who it was; perhaps it was the possibility of distraction, something to take her mind off Edward and Nicholas. She peeked into the room and saw Rory sitting on the lounge suite, his head on the back rest, his eyes on the ceiling, quite a regular pose for him. He held a glass of clear liquid in his hand and his jaw trembled.

She tried to back out softly but hit the edge of the wall with the heel of her foot, and Rory's head jerked up.

'Alex,' he called. 'Hello.'

'Sorry,' she said, not quite knowing what to say and embarrassed that she'd caught him in this candid moment. 'I heard something and ...'

'Come and sit with me,' he said, gesturing to the seat opposite the centre table.

Alex didn't feel comfortable about it, the incident with Samuel springing to mind, but she did as she was asked, something drawing her there. 'Where's Cheryl?' she asked, looking at the clock, which showed seven p.m. She usually didn't come back inside until after twelve, sometimes one.

'Netty's having a … a bad day.'

'Anything I can do to help?'

Rory shrugged his shoulders and raised his glass in question. Alex shook her head and tucked her hands under her thighs. Her eyes scanned the room, so rustic in the glow of the lamp in the corner of the room, yet so lonely. She shivered involuntarily.

'Are you cold?'

'No,' she replied. She was a little chilly, the night air still on her cheeks.

'It gets cold in here. Apart from the fireplace and the portable heaters, there's not much in the way of heating.

'Cheryl got me one for my room, so it's fine.'

'I just can't get myself to install modern amenities here. I want to keep this place as it was.' He shook his head in resignation. 'Not for long though.' He sniffed. 'Not if Sam has anything to do with it.'

Alex nodded, not knowing how to respond. She wished she hadn't stopped.

'So, tell me, Alex.' He leaned back, took a sip of his drink and surveyed her. 'What's your story?' Alex was a little taken aback, and Rory smiled at her startled expression.

'This is pretty much what it is. I'm no great mystery.' She thought it a strange question now, months after she arrived here.

He hesitated. 'You're back early tonight.' His eyes seemed to dance now.

'Oh.' She thought about Edward fading before her and a sudden chill came upon her.

'What do you do out there every night?'

'I don't know,' she said. She thought her whereabouts every evening went unnoticed in the dark of winter's evening. 'I just …'

He clearly wasn't going to let her off. He watched her, a wicked smile dancing on his lips, and Alex reddened.

'I just like walking the grounds. It's so peaceful.'

'And so cold.'

'You go out every evening too,' she countered, remembering that he rode his horse every night.

'Yes, true,' he said and stopped. 'But I don't come back

in the early hours of the morning.'

Alex was dumbfounded. She really didn't realise what she did was so acutely observed. She shrugged.

'I've seen you, many times,' he said and her jaw fell slightly. 'No, don't be embarrassed.' He leaned forward again. 'If you want to use the gazebo for your dancing then that's fine.'

'You've … you've seen me dance in there?'

He nodded and looked down into his glass.

'You watched me?'

'I didn't mean to,' he said sheepishly. 'The first time I saw you, I was just, I don't know, mesmerised. You were just sliding across the floor.' He cleared his throat. 'It was quite beautiful actually.'

'You should have said something,' Alex replied.

'I didn't watch you after that but I saw you on my way back to the house a few times. I didn't want to be a weird voyeur.'

'Thanks,' she muttered.

'I didn't know you danced.'

'I guess there's not much to tell. Haven't done it for a long time.' She shrugged.

'We have a dance hall in the house, you know.' He raised his eyebrows.

'I've seen it.' She stared back at him in defiance.

'It's fine,' he said, chuckling. 'None of my business what you do. It's just that it's kinda creepy out there at night—beautiful, but still a little eerie.' He looked around him. 'Even in here sometimes. Especially lately.' He looked at her again. 'Just something, I don't know, strange; I can't explain it.'

Alex was interested now. She leaned forward. 'Strange? In what way?'

His eyes narrowed. 'Why do you ask?'

She straightened back to her cool self. 'Nothing, it's just interesting, that's all.'

'Why the gazebo?' He just came out with it and Alex was rattled.

'What do you mean?'

'What is it about that place that takes you there so often?'

'It's just a beautiful place. You can see almost the whole grounds when you're in there. It's just …'

'Who do you talk to?'

'Myself,' she said immediately and wondered where she got that answer from so quickly.

He nodded slowly. 'You are lonely.' It was a statement, not a question, and Alex didn't respond. 'I can see that.'

Alex rose to leave. This conversation was taking a bend she didn't want to go around and it was better to end it here. 'I need to go to bed.'

'Early for you,' he said, a twinkle in his eye. 'Hey, Alex,' he said as she turned to leave, and she paused. 'What will you do if he sells?'

'What do you mean?'

'If Samuel sells this place and we're forced to leave. Where will you go?'

'I don't know.' She wondered whether she should ask for his help now, when there was a clear opening.

'He's hoping to bring in buyers for the estate in December.'

'Why December anyway?' She'd been curious since Samuel mentioned it.

He smirked. 'You should see this place in December. The sun rises over the hill and casts a shadow and it's just …' He inhaled deeply. 'I can't even think of the right word for it.'

'Breathtaking?'

He laughed. 'Yes, that's probably the closest word. But right through until mid-January, we get people coming from all over asking if we're selling. Sometimes tourists, just on the way through. There's a picture in the pub of the house and people are curious. And now Sam wants to take advantage of it.'

Alex nodded, thinking of Edward. What would become of Edward?

'He didn't tell you when he hired you, did he?'

'No.'

'He should have at least warned you. But he's sneaky too. I wouldn't give him permission, so he went with an ongoing person, thinking he was throwing me off track. I let him just to shut him up, but …'

'Why didn't you tell me?'

'Because I'm still living in hope that we will beat him. That we can convince him to keep it. But it's half his and I can't buy him out. Not on my salary anyway.'

'I'm sorry,' said Alex. 'Where will you go?'

'Haven't decided yet. Not a lot of time to think or talk about it.' He looked down at his glass and frowned. 'Besides, it may even be a good time for a change.' He looked around again now. 'Leave all this behind.'

Alex knew he was talking about Netty and her heart softened at his plight. Leaving behind a house that they'd raised their family in, and leaving it without one of its members. But she knew about leaving things behind and wasn't sure if it was working for her.

'By the way, I have that number for you.' He reached into his jacket that lay on the arm of his chair. He rummaged in the pocket and pulled out a piece of paper. 'Here it is.'

'I …' She reached forward, grabbed the paper and looked at the familiar scrawl of Nicholas. 'Thanks.'

'Who is he?'

'Nobody,' she replied. 'A part of my past. Something that should remain there,' she said almost to herself and was surprised it came out so Rory heard it. She hurried out of the room before he could respond.

September 30

Dear Mum and Pa,

I have all this happening and I'm still so desperately lonely. I don't know why I'm here right now. I hurt Edward today. I said awful things to him. I wanted to hurt him, I don't know why. Maybe because he will go if I do. Then I can get on with trying to be normal, whatever that is. I can't imagine him not being here though. And what about Nicholas? I saw him today and I don't think I feel any less for him. I think I'm still in love with him. It took all my strength to leave him there, back in Melbourne, and today in Chernut. Can I go back? I don't know anymore.

She raised her head and looked out the window, but couldn't discern anything, the moon completely covered with clouds, and her heart sank. Maybe he was gone ... for good. No! She couldn't believe that. She thought about going out again, but her mood was still sad and she would just ruin it all again. She had to sleep on it tonight and let whatever happened, happen. It was an unsettling thought, she always needed to have control of what happened; she'd never left anything up to fate. Not after that night so long ago.

Sweet dreams, miss you xx

CHAPTER 21

'I'm sorry,' said Cheryl, sniffing.

'It's okay,' replied Alex, patting her on her back, not knowing what else to do.

'I want to, Alex, I really do.' She broke into a fresh bout of sobs. 'But I feel like slapping him when he comes near me.'

'But why? You say you love him.'

'Oh, I do,' she cried. 'I do so, so much!'

'Does he know that?'

'I ...'

'Tell him.'

'I just can't. I just resent him sometimes. Like, why are you thinking about having sex with me when our little girl is ...' Another gush of tears.

'You need to get through this together.'

'I don't want to get through anything!'

'You have a man who loves you, another little girl who adores you, and a teenage daughter who sees and understands everything you do.'

'What do you mean?'

'She just wants her mother to be happy. She can see that you're not and blames herself for it.'

'I haven't done …'

'I know. But she talks about when you and Rory used to dance together and were happy and she says you're not anymore. Please don't tell her I said anything.'

'I didn't realise.'

'No, of course you didn't.' Alex patted her hand. 'Just be as happy as you can. Take it with both hands, whatever you can. Hold on to it.' She stopped, wondering there that came from. That certainly wasn't anything she felt herself.

'But I don't even know how anymore.' Cheryl took her head out of her hands. 'Tell me what I can do?' She sounded hopeful, too hopeful to be looking for advice from Alex, who didn't feel like she was in any position to give anyone advice on love.

She absently set aside her hoe and looked around. She hadn't seen him in days.

'Alex?' She heard Cheryl call, but her ears were buzzing now. Thoughts of Nicholas and Edward rushed through her head, their voices, not saying anything, echoing loud in her ears.

'Alex?'

Alex turned back to Cheryl, who was leaning towards her in concern. 'Sorry ...'

'You just went far away.' She put her hand to her mouth. 'I'm sorry, I'm just blabbing on and you must have your own problems.'

'I'm okay,' said Alex, shaking her head free of the images that had just invaded her brain.

'You can talk to me, too, you know,' said Cheryl.

Alex nodded. 'I will. I know.'

When Cheryl left, Alex stood there in the dimming light, wishing he would come to her and also hoping he wouldn't. She walked gingerly to the gazebo and stood at the entrance, her fingers sliding over the smooth wooden poles. The setting sun was visible on the far end and she wished it were filled with the silhouette of Edward now. She wanted him to come to her, wanted to feel his arms around her, his lips on hers, his feet sliding her off the floor in a dance.

Moving to the centre of the floor, she closed her eyes and turned around, her arms lifting slowly in the air. Then she was spinning again and again, the music was playing and she was on her toes. It came back so easily, the way her foot defied her body, rising to the ceiling effortlessly, her fingers reaching for the edge of her boot, her head falling backward with ease. She felt his arm touch the back of her waist and she curled her body forward into his embrace, her eyes still closed. She felt his leg guide hers backward, and she let herself be led to the rise of the tempo. Across the floor she spun, in a daze, the clarity of his being too clear to be anything but real. Before she knew it, his lips were on hers, his hands pushing her chin to his face, and she was clutching his back so tightly, she didn't want him to ever leave her again.

Opening her eyes, she leaned back and saw his eyes open, gazing at her with such a ferocity of tenderness, she felt chills of fear run up her neck. It was the same. He wanted more than she could give. But this time it was she who wanted more and Edward who couldn't give it.

CHAPTER 22

Alex sipped at her coffee, a frown on her face, her fingers tapping the tabletop nervously. Even after a magical evening with Edward, her heart was split in two. But he had walked with her and they had become themselves again, talking under the moon, admiring the flowers.

'What's your story, Edward?' she had asked, realising she didn't know much about him at all. 'Did you have a wife? A girlfriend?'

His eyes had clouded. 'I loved once.'

Alex had waited for more and she looked at Edward, whose lips were pursed, his frowning eyes straight ahead of them. 'That's cryptic.'

'There was only ever one woman who had my heart.'

After all this time, he still wasn't ready to share himself with her. *For that matter,* she thought, *neither am I.* She wondered why that was. Maybe they just didn't want to break the spell that kept them bonded. Maybe they were both living in a fantasy world, loving other people, trying to forget them.

'Would you like to hear something amusing?' He was changing the subject and Alex had been disappointed. 'I did a very ghostly thing. I think you might like it.' His eyes had been twinkling.

'Oh? Tell me,' she had said, nudging his arm.

'That awful man, Samuel, the one you don't have very nice words for …'

Alex had frowned. 'What about him?'

'I was waiting for you. It was yesterday …' He had looked thoughtful. 'Perhaps more time has gone by.'

'Yes, anyway,' Alex had said impatiently.

'Well, I was waiting for you and he walked past the house. I know he did something to you, so I thought I may play a game with him.'

'Oh Edward! Tell me!' Alex had been surprised at her enthusiasm.

'It was quite early and he walked through the hedge.' He had pointed to the hedge by the back of the house. 'I know I can't touch a lot of things, but I opened my mouth and let out a howl, a ghoulish howl.' He had laughed. 'I think it worked because the man looked up and I could see he was terrified. He ran straight into the house.'

'Oh Edward!' Alex had said again, tickled at his playful side. She had mentioned to Edward that Samuel was not a nice man and although she didn't tell him what had happened that night Samuel had been a lech, she had alluded to it, and as dead as Edward was, he wasn't stupid. People were lecherous back in the 1940s too, she guessed. Besides, he had probably seen Samuel eye Alex a few times in the garden too.

'I hope we won't see him lurking about out here anymore.' Edward had crossed his arms, a satisfied grin on his face.

Alex bit on her toast now, taking more time than usual to go out today. She was thoughtful. Sure, Samuel got a little payback for his bad behaviour, but that could mean more. He would certainly push for the sale of the house with even more vehemence now. She sighed. December was not far away. Either way, time was running out.

Cathy burst into the kitchen, her plate of breakfast in her hand, and placed herself on a stool next to Alex. 'Mama is taking me out,' she announced, a grin on her face.

Alex looked down in amusement at the little head that bobbed up and down in excitement. 'Oh? Where are you going?'

'I think to the sea,' she said through the spluttering of a mouthful of scrambled eggs. Alex raised her eyebrows and the girl looked up at her, her eyes sparkling with happiness. The beach was more than an hour away and Alex was surprised. The family rarely left the house any further than Chernut. In all the time Alex had been at Lovelet Manor, only once had she known Cheryl to leave the house for more than an hour and she'd come home in the afternoon carting a large plastic bag, which Netty had told her was a new console for her games. But to take Cathy out? That hadn't happened in the five months Alex had been here. 'Yep, just me and Mama.'

Alex smiled. Cheryl had heeded her advice. She ruffled Cathy's hair and the girl's smile grew wider. 'Make sure you have fun. Oh, and eat lots of ice cream, it's going to be a warm one today.'

Cathy finished her meal and bounded out of the room. 'Gotta go,' she said as the door opened, Cheryl moving past quickly to avoid the hurricane that was her youngest child.

'She's excited,' said Alex.

'Yes, she is.' Cheryl stood by the end of the bench and twiddled her fingers together, her brows knitted.

'Are you okay?' Alex could see she was unsure of what she was doing.

'Yes, yes, I think so.'

'What's the matter? You don't look as excited as Cathy.'

'Yes, I am.' She looked up but above her smiling lips were eyes filled with worry. 'But …'

'Are you worried about Netty?'

'Angela is coming over to spend the day with her.' Angela, who Netty seemed to have a love-hate relationship with. 'But …'

'She is fond of Angela. It should be fine.' She moved to Cheryl and twiddled her own fingers. 'You should go. Don't let Cathy down. Don't make excuses not to try to enjoy yourself either.'

The scared eyes looked at her, attempting to brighten.

'And whatever you do, don't feel guilty! Besides, it might be nice for Netty to have a break from you too, you know.' She laughed and Cheryl snickered. 'If it helps, I could spend some time with her this afternoon? I have less of a load this morning and I was going to just tidy up a little.' Alex didn't have less work. In fact, she had a lot to catch up with; she hadn't been on her best game lately and was trying to work longer hours to make up for it.

Cheryl's eyes lit up as if she were waiting for Alex to

offer. 'Would you? She'd love that and I wouldn't worry about her as much. She loves it when you visit her. And then I wouldn't have to cut the day short too. And Rory should be back around four thirty, so he can take over.' She was babbling and Alex put her hand on her arm.

'Yes, it's fine. I don't have much to do anyway.' She was thinking about the time she would spend with Edward that would have to be cut short as well.

'Thanks, Alex,' said Cheryl, a sigh of relief escaping her lips.

'No problem,' she said. 'Have fun.' She headed to the back door and turned around. 'Oh, and make sure you buy Cathy the ice cream I promised her,' she said, winking, and Cheryl laughed.

She breathed in the crisp morning air that wafted to her as she opened the door and smiled. It always made her smile. Spring was already displaying its presence, the withery leaves of winter opening to numerous shades of green. Yet it was still cold, the chill in the air hard to get used to on such pleasant days when the sun burned bright from early morning to mid-evening. But the arrival of spring just brought her closer to her fate, whatever that was.

Frowning now, Alex went to the shed to collect the equipment she would need for the morning and headed to the far end of the gardens, where she told Edward she would be working today. He had smiled and told her he would meet her there and her heart quickened as it always did when she thought about seeing him. But Nicholas's visit had unnerved her and thoughts of him ran through her mind often now, thoughts she didn't banish as easily as she had before. His face, his laugh, his words. And how she felt safe wrapped in his arms in bed, and the fear that made her move away to the far side of it. Their shared love of pasta and their shared hate of sushi, and the argument over which was better, Pepsi or Coke, and the evenings they spent walking around the lake, Nicholas trying to convince her to get a dog, and Alex not conceding—a dog would only tie them together and would only be another thing to worry about losing.

She looked over at Scamper, who sat every day next to the stables, with the horses, his head resting on his paws, but his big brown eyes alert. She patted his head every time she walked past and he'd raise his head and shake his tail from side to side and then put his head back on his paws. He was old and it wouldn't be very long before he would be gone too. No, she was right to refuse to have a dog. She looked at Scamper and he raised his eyebrows at her. Alex put her hand under his chin and scratched, watching the dog's eyes close in ecstasy, and wondered if she had been wrong. Maybe Nicholas had been right, maybe she needed to be more attached to things, not fear them ... Hopefully he had gotten himself the dog, once she had left. What if he'd found someone else? She wished he didn't; the thought of him moving on so quickly sent chills through her and another pang of guilt hit her as she imagined his face, filled with sorrow if he knew about Edward. But he came to find her. For the first time, she wondered whether she had been wrong to leave. She knew how close she had come to saying yes to his proposal. And yet …

She took a deep breath and got into the buggy, driving straight to the fence line. Samuel would probably be irritated if he knew she was working on it. It was too far away from the main house to be noticed and she knew he would feel it was a waste of time. She smiled at her little act of defiance against that horrid man.

'Hello, dearest Alexandra.' His voice floated down to her as it usually did every day and she turned to see him bent to her, his hand held out, palm up as it usually was. She took off her glove and offered him the back of her hand, which he took and held his lips to for a moment.

It was quite natural now for him to appear, wander with her while she worked and chat about the weather and other inconsequential things, none of them discussing the arrival of December, less than two months away now. Sometimes she talked about the family and sometimes they didn't talk at all. By now Alex knew she had to work harder to keep up with the chores she set for herself and at times Edward was a distraction. She tried to resist kissing him, knowing she would be taken by his spell and whenever Edward got too close, breathing words of nothing into her ear, she'd playfully push him away, knowing how easily she could be swayed by him.

'I just want to be near you,' he protested when he put his hand on her hand, running his fingers up her arm.

'Yes, me too, but I have to work. There's plenty of time for that later.' She shook him off.

'Later seems a long way away.' She could see he was trying not to pout and enjoyed the effect she had on him.

'It will make you want me more,' she said, surprised at her coquetry, and he raised his eyebrows.

And so it went, Alex keeping her impulses at bay until the evening, after she went back to the house, scrubbed herself, delicately applied mascara and a dash of lipstick, threw on a dress, a coat if it were a very cold evening, and one of the only two pairs of dress shoes she owned, left untouched until she met Edward. Then she'd stop in to check on Netty, sometimes stay with her for a little while, and go to the gazebo, where Edward would already be waiting for her, his straight-backed figure, one hand behind his back, in the entrance framed by the glistening pink sky behind him.

Her heart would always skip a beat at the sight of him and he would hold out his hand to receive her. Then they would walk the grounds or sit and watch the sun fully set, his arm around her, her head resting on his shoulder. Inevitably there would be a dance which Alex now looked forward to. And just as inevitably he would kiss her when she departed for the night. But that was as far as it went and Alex, as much as she knew she felt so much for him, knew that was as far as it could go, not physically, she had no idea how that would even work, but emotionally, she knew she couldn't.

Alex wondered why she let him in so fully into her heart now and suspected it was because she already knew it was not to last. She was expecting heartbreak already; it was not something she could avoid, his leaving, or her leaving. She just hoped that he wouldn't disappear without her knowing, that she might have some preparation, but she realised she was already preparing.

Now, she smiled at him, having done a short twirl around the gazebo.

'When will you show me your own dances?' Edward said unexpectedly. So far, she had been waltzing with him, doing the quickstep and the foxtrot, and when in an especially sad mood, Alex would just lean on Edward while he moved about the floor, his hand on her head which rested against his chest.

'You want to dance my dances?'

'Why, yes,' he said in adamance.

Alex wasn't so sure she wanted to return to that place. 'Well, there's the ballet …'

Edward looked down at his shoes and frowned.

'There's also the jive, which my parents taught me and which I performed sometimes,' she hurried on, understanding his reluctance.

He smiled triumphantly. 'I've heard of that one.'

'There are also some extremely sexy Latin numbers …'

'You will have to show me,' he said, beaming. 'But I cannot guarantee that I will be able to perform those newfangled styles.'

'I have to leave early today,' she said ruefully and his mouth straightened. 'Cheryl needs a favour. I'll try to return tonight, but I'm not sure when I will be able to or if I will.'

'If you return, I will be here,' he said.

CHAPTER 23

Alex could hear Netty yelling as she neared her room and rushed forward. 'You are annoying me! Why don't you mind your business?'

'Annette …'

'Don't call me that!'

'Netty …'

'Stop calling me that …' Netty looked up at the appearance of Alex and gave her an angry stare, crossing her arms stubbornly as she did.

Alex looked around to see Angela, a bowl in her hands, trying to barricade with her arms against the objects that Netty had obviously been throwing at her. A pillow, a mug, a plush elephant, none that were close to hitting their target. Netty just didn't have the strength. 'Netty! Stop it,' Alex said and moved to the bed.

Netty, looking more pale than usual, turned her head to the other side, avoiding Alex's glare. Alex turned to Angela and raised her brows.

'She was meant to eat half an hour ago,' the woman said helplessly. 'She was fine before and then she …'

'Don't talk about me like I'm not here,' shrieked Netty and Angela cowered, awaiting another projectile.

'Here,' said Alex, taking the bowl from Angela. 'Take a break. I wanted to spend some time with her anyway.'

'You too,' said Netty, turning to Alex. 'Don't talk about me.' She pouted, her arms still crossed.

'And you,' Alex said to Netty after Angela had handed the bowl to her and scurried out of the room. 'Stop acting like a child. Eat your damned food.' She looked into the bowl to see a broth that looked the colour of pee and which smelled not much better. 'What on earth is this?' she asked, taking a sniff and wrinkled her nose.

Netty giggled involuntarily. 'I'll have some if you do too,' she said triumphantly and broke out into a bout of coughs which Alex ignored. She never acknowledged the weakness of Netty, sometimes just passing her a tissue if she observed any blood spatter. There was none this time but she waited for the coughing to stop and for Netty to compose herself.

'Ick. No thanks.' She looked at Netty. 'Is this part of a diet or something?'

'No!'

'Well, why are you having this?'

'I don't know. That's what I was asking when she tried to make me have it.'

'This is not Milly's food.'

'No, it is not!'

'Well, if you wait a few minutes, I'll get rid of this … stuff, and bring you something more edible.'

Alex returned to Netty's room with a piece of roast chicken and baked potatoes, which she diced before bringing it up, and a sheepish grin.

'You would think that they'd serve me something good for the rest of my very short life, even if I can't really enjoy it. It should be like a last meal every meal because it just might be,' she said as she poked her fork into the food. 'What was with that muck?'

'I think Milly was busy with the upstairs rooms and Angela didn't want to bother her, so she poured what she thought was soup. It really was broth, the same that Milly used for the chicken.' She laughed as Netty giggled too. 'And stop this crap about last meals. I hope you don't go around saying that to your mother all the time.'

'As you may have noticed,' said Netty, raising her head, 'I don't "go around" anywhere.'

'You know what I meant. Stop being morbid. You're not getting a rise out of me, young lady. I'm not as nice as Angela.'

'Is she upset?' Netty looked apologetic now.

'She understands. I told her about the broth and she's so embarrassed but promise me you won't tease her about it.'

'Yes, okay. By the way, my last meal was not a joke. I think it's time soon.' She looked around. 'I've been wanting to talk to you about it. I just don't know how …'

Alex pulled up the chair and placed herself on it, steeling herself for what may come next. More news from the doctor, perhaps, but Netty had been looking good lately; well, as good as she ever did.

'I think it's time,' Netty repeated.

'Time for what?' asked Alex, knowing exactly what Netty meant.

'To go.'

Alex leaned back in her chair and folded her arms.

'Okay?'

'I don't even know how to explain it.' Netty twirled her fork in her fingers and stared at her plate.

Alex remained still but a shiver crept slowly up her spine.

'I think there's something … someone …'

The shiver kept moving up Alex's spine and tingled her ears.

Netty shook her head and placed a piece of chicken in her mouth. 'It's stupid,' she mumbled. 'I know you humour me sometimes.'

Alex waited for her to finish chewing which seemed to take forever. 'Whatever it is, I'm sure it's not stupid.'

Netty put her plate on the table beside her and leaned forward. 'I feel something, Alex. No, not just feel something. I think there's someone around.' She looked furtively around the room.

'What do you mean?'

'Like a ghost.' She rolled her eyes. 'I know, sounds stupid, right?'

Her stomach in knots now, Alex propped her elbows on the bed. 'Tell me more.'

Netty squinted her eyes at Alex. 'Are you making fun of me?'

'No. I want to hear more.' Alex could feel her heart beating fast now.

Netty, with some trouble, brought her legs up and crossed them, her eyes too bright against her pallid face. 'So, I have been having this feeling for a few months now. Like someone is watching me. Not all the time, but usually when I'm by myself.' She turned up her eyes in thought. 'Not always when I'm by myself, but mostly. Just a weird feeling. And then, because of my being sick, I thought maybe I'm just being … you know, sick. Like maybe that's what's supposed to happen.' She paused. 'Like hallucinations or whatever.'

Alex could feel her forehead becoming moist and her mouth filled with saliva. She swallowed. 'Keep going, Netty,' she urged.

'Okay, and then I thought maybe I was paranoid, because it happens mostly at night. Like really late at night when everyone is asleep.' She paused. 'I wake up often, you know that.'

'Keep going,' said Alex, when Netty stopped to take a breath. 'Sorry, take your time.' She realised it was a struggle for Netty to talk for an extended period of time.

'No, it's fine. I need to talk to someone about it.' She

twirled the ends of her sheet in her skeletal fingers. 'Anyway, I got used to it. But then lately, I have been seeing things,' she said, looking into Alex's eyes, and Alex nodded to reassure her that she believed her. 'Shadows, things moving past, not even quick, just moving. And then last night, Alex …' she said, and Alex saw a quick shiver run through Netty. 'I saw him. I saw him but I wasn't scared of him.'

Alex swallowed again and leaned in closer. 'What did he look like?'

'He wasn't very clear, but he was tall, I know he had a suit on and a white shirt. And he smiled at me, Alex; it was so nice. And I wasn't scared at all,' she repeated, almost as if to reassure Alex that it was okay to have a lurking ghost in her bedroom.

'Did he say anything?'

'I think so. But it was like it was blurry, you know, like a blurry screen, but it was his voice. It was rough …'

Alex didn't need to know more. In fact she didn't need to know more than when Netty began her story. Her eyes filled.

'It's okay, Alex. I told you I'm ready,' said Netty, misunderstanding her tears. 'I think he's come to help me. I'm not frightened.'

'Oh Netty, how are you so brave?' Alex realised that's

not what she should have been saying to a dying girl, but she couldn't understand how someone knew their time was coming and was okay with it.

Netty laughed cynically. 'I prepared my whole life for this. It's like training for the Olympics. And it's finally here.' She sobered her expression. 'Do you think I'm seeing and hearing things?'

'No, I don't.'

'Are you just saying that?'

'No. I believe you did see and hear him.'

'Is it in my head?'

'No, Netty, I don't think that either.'

Netty looked relieved. 'Okay.' She grabbed her plate back and began to cut into her chicken again, which was probably cold by now. 'Let's watch *Dirty Dancing* again,' she said and Alex picked up the remote to select the movie. 'Oh, and Alex?' She stopped mid-munch. 'He was older, but he was cute.'

Dear Mum and Pa,

I think he's here for Netty, not for me. And as much as I feel—I don't know the word—rejected, maybe? No, not that. I know he loves me already, but I don't know why he came to me then. I think I want to ask him about it, but he hasn't said anything either. Wait, maybe he doesn't know? Maybe there's two of him? Or two versions? Oh gosh, I don't know a thing anymore. Tell you more when I know more. Love you.

Alex hadn't gone back out the previous evening after her visit with Netty, and after writing to her parents, she walked to the window and looked towards the gazebo, seeing its glow, trying to resist the urge to run to him. It was early when Cheryl and Cathy returned from their trip, Cathy elated, sand particles stuck to her hair. Cheryl burst into Netty's room, panic-stricken, and her body shuddered in relief when she saw Netty and Alex munching on popcorn. 'It's the end, Mum, come back in ten,' Netty had said, and Alex winked at Cheryl, who smiled shakily and backed out of the room.

Alex couldn't bring herself to ask Edward about it, not right away, but she steeled herself to talk to him about it the next day on their evening stroll and suddenly, she realised she didn't know much about him at all! They had been spending almost every waking hour together and she'd never enquired about his past. Of course, he talked about the manor, about how he built it and how he'd designed the gardens, even though some of it had been changed, but their conversations were never consequential, they had been too rapt in each other's presence to think about anything more. Now she realised that she may have been too afraid of what she would hear.

CHAPTER 24

'Could I have the morning off?'

Rory looked up from the breakfast table, where he had been dining alone today, in surprise. 'Why?'

'I need to run an errand,' Alex continued. 'You can dock my pay, it's fine.'

Rory gave her an amused smile. 'No, I don't mean why, as in why. I meant, I hope you're okay. You don't leave here too often.'

'I just have to go to the post office,' she said, looking down at her thumbs which she was twiddling in nervousness. She couldn't imagine explaining her errand to Rory.

'Yes, fine, no problem.' His eyes looked worriedly at her. 'You don't need to ask, Alex. You work much more than you are supposed to.'

'Thanks,' she said and turned to leave.

'Are you okay? Really?'

'Yep, fine.'

She may not have felt the same sense of dread as she did when she first left the manor, but knowing Edward was waiting for her, she still felt a sliver of guilt. She parked at the post office and looked around. The town hall, which she had not really noticed before, stood just a little way away, a quaint, faded-yellow building, Chernut plastered on the front, just above its yellowed doors. Alex swallowed and got out of the car. She stood beside it, her hand still on the open door, feeling like she was snooping. Why couldn't she just ask him about his life? Why did she have to find out about him by going to the archives? She may not find anything here anyway.

The moment she stepped into the hall, she saw it. Her throat tightened and she floated towards the giant photograph on the opposite end of the wall.

'Can I help you?'

Alex jumped and turned to see an older man, perhaps in his late sixties, his head cocked to one side in question, sitting at a lone table to her right.

'Er,' Alex stammered. 'I'm Alex, Alexandra. I just wanted to know the history of the er, Chernut … and Lovelet Manor.'

'Well, you've come to the right place then!' The man beamed and shuffled backwards in his seat and came over to Alex, a limp in his walk. 'I'm Terry. Been here since I was born. Know everything there is to know about Chernut, town and village. I've been here since the day my mother birthed me.' He held out his hand and Alex shook the little fingers. Terry was a head shorter than she was and Alex tried to crouch to make herself look shorter. 'Have you been to the manor?'

Alex wasn't sure whether or not to tell him the truth. It would seem weird that she was coming to town to enquire about the house, rather than ask its occupants about it. But the man's smile was so genuine, she couldn't lie. 'I work there. I'm the gardener.'

'Oh, that Alex.'

Alex raised her eyebrows in surprise.

'Oh, don't worry, love,' he said reassuringly. 'Anyone new in town and, well, everyone knows about it.' He frowned. 'What do you need to know?' Alex wasn't so sure she wanted to ask anymore but she took another look at the serious face of Edward in the large photograph and Terry followed her gaze. 'Okay, let's start with him.'

Again, Alex felt guilty, like she was spying on him. 'Maybe start with the town,' she said.

'Well, that begins with him too,' replied Terry and shuffled towards the picture, which Alex didn't want to look at anymore. 'This town didn't exist, just a long stretch of road which led from Melbourne to Adelaide. Then came Edward Johns, all by himself, a young pecker, just nineteen at the time. As history says it, he fell out of favour with his father and was given a small sum of money and he rode around all over the place looking for the perfect spot to build his house.' Terry looked at Alex. 'The manor. Lovelet.'

Alex nodded, imagining Edward, a younger Edward on his horse in the middle of nowhere. 'Why here?'

'Apparently he set down for the night and while he was about to close his eyes for the night, he caught the light of dusk. He fell in love with it.'

Alex smiled. She found Edward gazing at the sunset on more than one occasion.

'So he put in a patent and off he went, building the house of his dreams. Then he built a garden and word got out, so people came from all over the place to see it. He put in a watering hole for the visitors, but then there were too many people, so he moved the pub to what is now Chernut Town.' Terry looked towards the door and waved his arm about. 'The name comes from cherry nut, the nubs on the end of the stalks, weeds really, that this area is famous for. There was a plantation of wheat. It's murky who created that. His father, I think. Maybe his brother, but who knows.' Terry shrugged. 'Anyway, then of course it expanded to the village and people moved here. Then of course the town exploded.'

'Okay,' said Alex, not feeling like there was anything remarkable about this story, her guilt lessening.

Terry waved about him. 'This was the dance hall that Edward Johns built. There were many dances and occasions held in here.' He turned to Alex. 'There's one in the manor too. Have you seen it?'

She nodded with a frown. Alex thought of the room that she had not gone into after her first day at the manor, the one that had made her weak, had sent back thoughts of her dancing days, of days she never imagined she'd go back to. And now she danced almost every day with Edward, life flowing back into her bones, doing what she used to love, the guilt swept away by the joy she felt in Edward's arms.

Edward. Here she was, prying into his life, trying to find out sneakily what she was too much of a coward to ask him herself.

'Rumour had it that …' Terry began.

'I have to go.' Alex touched the man's arm to stop him from going on and he gave her a surprised look. 'I have some errands to run,' she hurried on.

'But I thought you came to learn the history ...'

'Maybe another day,' said Alex, feeling sorry for the little man who clearly didn't have many enquiries about the history of the town that he had all the answers to, that he was so excited to share. But it was from Edward, she realised now, from whom she wanted to hear it.

She drove back to the manor after collecting a few items from the grocery store, including a new magazine for Netty and a chocolate bar for Cathy. As she parked her car, her phone buzzed and Alex jumped. It hadn't rung since she'd been here. She'd inserted a new SIM card and no one knew her number. She just kept it for safety reasons and in case she needed to google something for work. It only just occurred to her that she could get all the information she required about Edward from it. She dug into her handbag and retrieved it, seeing a number she didn't recognise, and wondered whether to answer it. The only numbers she had stored in it were Cheryl and Rory's, in case of emergency. Maybe it was Nicholas, maybe he had tracked her down, but she knew his number by heart. Her throat tightened and she stared at the screen until the buzzing stopped. She swallowed hard. Maybe it was a wrong number. Well, in that case there was no need to worry.

She pulled on the door handle and it rang again, the

same number, and Alex answered, more out of shock than curiosity. 'Hello?'

'Blanche!' Tom Sidebottom's voice shouted through the receiver.

Her heart dropped. She had been terrified it was Nicholas and now she was disappointed it wasn't. 'Hello, Mr Sidebottom,' she replied. Her father's lawyer's voice gave her an odd sense of soothing.

'Where have you been, Blanche? I've been searching for you. I was worried.'

Alex realised she should probably at least have told the old man where she was, but she didn't want to leave any trace of her whereabouts. 'I've moved. I'm okay.'

'Good, good.' She could hear the relief in his voice. 'It was a bugger to get your number. I searched everywhere, went to your place, some stranger living there didn't know a thing about where you were. I even went back to your dashed aunt's house.'

Alex's heart jumped. 'Don't give them my number,' she blurted.

'Of course not, what do you take me for?' She could hear him chuckle and smiled. 'But are you okay?'

'Yes, yes, I'm, fine.' She wondered why he was calling. 'Are you?'

'I'm well, thank you for asking. I was making my regular call to you, to see if you had changed your mind about your trust.'

'Oh,' said Alex, relieved. Mr Sidebottom called her a couple of times a year just to check on her. But in August every year, he called to settle her finances, always asking if she needed to know the balance. She never wanted to. 'No. Can we leave it?' It was the same conversation every time.

'As you wish.' She heard him sigh. 'Where are you living now?'

Alex knew she could trust him. 'A few hours from Melbourne, a little town called Chernut.'

'Hmm, never heard of it,' he said. Alex smiled. Just as she hoped. But Nicholas had found her here. 'Oh, I also spoke to your friend, Nicholas. I tracked him down at the nursery. He is very worried about you.'

Her heart almost stopped. 'Please don't tell him where I am.'

'Why? Did he do something? Is that why you left?' She could hear his voice harden.

'No, not at all. I … I just had to leave Melbourne and Melbourne was also Nicholas. I just want to live alone, in peace, where I am,' she said, unsure she believed what she was saying.

'Okay.' His voice was tired. 'Just reassure me that you are okay.'

'I am, and thank you for hunting me down. I should have let you know where I was.'

'Yes, you should have,' he said sternly. 'But you're forgiven. Please let me know if you need anything … I mean, anything, Blanche.'

'I will, thanks, Mr Sidebottom.' He'd given up trying to make her call him Tom.

She hung up and clicked to her contacts. She'd put his number in—he was the only person who had a connection to her parents, the only one she trusted, anyway. She should have remembered to do it beforehand, then she wouldn't be so disappointed. She leaned her head on the rest and closed her eyes. She was tired. Not her body but her mind, her heart. She left Melbourne to escape the fear of heartbreak but it surrounded her in this place. Yet this she could bear, the certainty of loss, of death. But was it any better?

****

A light sprinkling of rain touched the grass, and Alex looked up at the sky. It had been another bright day, but the sparse white clouds had gained momentum, turning to grey before her very eyes. She hesitated at the kitchen door and turned back to Milly, who was eyeing her with a knowing look. She had on more than one occasion asked Alex what she did out there every evening and Alex always told her she liked walking the grounds, which she reasoned wasn't a lie. Before Edward, she'd even gone past the fence line, over to the edge of the river, where she dipped her feet in, watching the swans gliding over the water or the frogs lazing in the sun, and sometimes she just looked over the horizon, letting that feeling of calm envelop her as this place always did. But since Edward, every minute without him was a waste of that minute and she hadn't been to the river for some months now, except when she ran in the mornings.

Alex shrugged and hurried out. She hesitated again and walked to the shed where she found one of the horses gone. She patted Shoret and rested her head on his nose and took a deep breath. She had to face him.

CHAPTER 25

'So all I know about your, er, life …'—Alex didn't quite know how to put it, but the left side of Edward's lip rose in a teasing curl—'is that you were a dancer, a professional dancer, and that you, er, left at forty.'

'You don't need to be careful with me, Alexandra,' he said, squeezing her hand, and she entwined her fingers in his.

'Alexandra?' He nudged her ribs lightly.

'Why do you call me that?'

'Why, that's your name, is it not?'

'Well, it is.' She thought of her real name and wondered if she should tell him. 'But I'm called Alex by everyone.'

'You first introduced yourself to me as Alexandra.'

'Did I?' She still couldn't remember clearly what had happened when they first met.

He nodded and then frowned. 'Are you okay, Alexandra … Alex?'

She put her hand on his arm, feeling she needed to reassure him, and they walked further up the path towards the fence line in silence. The drizzle had subsided, and Alex watched as the droplets of water glistened on the pink roses that lined this side of the fence. She resisted the urge to pluck one from its stem and she leaned on the fence and looked towards the endless hills of green that spread beyond the grounds.

'I want to stay here forever,' she said, almost to herself. Edward was silent and Alex turned around to see him look into the distance, his back straight as it always was, a look of yearning crinkling his eyes. 'Edward?'

'My father was disappointed in me,' said Edward, not turning to her, his gait unchanging. Alex remained silent, waiting for more. 'He was the mayor of Taraton, not a hundred miles from Chernut. He wanted me to stay there with my elder brother Joseph and take a position at the local council, but I had to leave.' Edward clenched his jaw and Alex was unsure of what to do. He looked down at Alex and smiled, and she took his hand.

He looked towards the shed now, where Shoret's head could be seen, peering in the distance at them, and Alex was concerned that Rory may come back from his ride. She took Edward's hand and guided him in the opposite direction. They walked in silence, their steps in sync, and Alex wondered if she should urge him to continue, but she needn't have.

'She taught me to dance. Eleanor.' Alex's throat caught. She'd seen the name on one of the gravestones. 'It was 1923 and I was in love with her. She was in love with me. We were the talk of the town. Do you know we won every competition we entered?' He gave a little chuckle of pride.

Alex wanted to look into his eyes, to see his expression, to feel what he was feeling, but she didn't risk it. She needed to know more.

'But after my mother passed away … I was nineteen at the time, my father turned to his business, and I just didn't want to do what he wanted me to. Joseph had written that he was ready to join the council, but it wasn't for me.' He chuckled again, this time wryly. 'He called me a playboy. Me!'

'What did you do?' Alex licked her lips. She wanted to know more about Eleanor.

'Well, he told me to make something of myself and I chose to continue studying the construction industry.' He took his hand from Alex and sat on a garden bench, his back straight, his eyes still on the horizon. 'But I think he was embarrassed, not just because I wouldn't take up the position he wanted for me, but because I still danced. He called it a sissy pastime. To me, it wasn't a pastime.' He looked at Alex, his eyes boring into hers. 'I loved to dance; to me, it was a sport, an occupation, something I could make of myself.'

Alex smiled into his eyes. 'I know how that must have felt.'

'Yes, you would.' He squeezed her hand. 'I'm sorry if this story is boring.'

'No, not at all.' Alex was enthralled. Just the thought of living to dance ignited her bones, and she felt a connection to someone who felt as she had, as she did again.

'I will give you the abridged version.' He smiled and looked down at their fingers, entwined on his lap. 'He gave me part of my inheritance, told me to find my fortune, and I went. On my horse, like in a Western movie I'd seen once.' He guffawed and then he grew serious. 'I left Eleanor; she didn't want me to go, but I had to. I needed to make something of myself, become a man. I had to leave her but I promised to return and bring her to wherever I lay down my roots.'

Alex couldn't bring herself to look at Edward anymore, the pain in his face was visible. 'You don't have to go on,' she said softly.

He continued as if he hadn't heard her. 'But I left it too late. I built this house, set up everything for her and wrote her every month. She never wrote back, not after the first letter.'

'Why not?' Alex demanded. She found herself riled with this woman now.

'It was two years later, when I'd nearly finished. The house wasn't as big as it is now, but it had a dance hall and I imagined us spending every evening in there, just swaying …' He suddenly broke from his reverie.

'It's okay, keep going,' said Alex, squeezing his hand and swallowing the saliva in her mouth.

'I wrote my father to visit when it was complete and he assured me he would come and bring my brother too. I was so terribly excited to see them after all that time. I was lonely. I asked after Eleanor but there was no answer on my father's part. Instead, when they came, my father and Joseph, Eleanor came with them, a ring on her finger.'

Alex gasped. She already knew.

'They were already married, but I knew she still loved me and I loved her too.'

'Oh Edward!'

'She never explained why she did it, but I knew. She wanted a serious life. And as much as she loved to dance, it was not serious enough for a man of my age.' He got off the bench and headed to the gazebo. He ran his hands over the wooden handrail. 'I built this for her, but she never saw it. She died in childbirth, leaving a child, a boy, Rory.'

She wanted to ask the obvious but didn't want to offend him.

'It was my child, but I couldn't see him, couldn't hold him like he was my own. He was my brother's.'

There was a sharp intake of breath from Alex, even though she guessed. 'Oh Edward,' she managed to say.

'I tried to stay away to work on the garden, work on the buildings. I stayed out of the grounds, extending the business, which ironically became the main earnings of my family. I finally made my father proud.'

'What happened?' Alex wanted to know more about what happened with Eleanor.

'She found me one evening.' He stroked the beam. 'It was here where she danced with me. She tried to explain again, but I still couldn't understand why she did it. We …' He looked skyward now.

Alex knew he was too gallant to mention the obvious. 'You made love?'

He nodded and gave a little cough. 'It was exactly nine months later.'

'Could it have been your brother's child?'

'No. I think Joseph knew it too. He had been away for a little while. He was still working with the council in Taranto and his job kept him away.'

'That would have left you and Eleanor time to …'

'No, my dear!' He sounded scandalised. 'We barely spoke. I admired her from afar, still in the belief that she was in love with my brother. Until that night.'

'What happened after that?'

'I threw myself into the garden and Joseph went mad. The child was raised by a nursemaid and by my father.'

'And you?'

'This is all I had.' He looked at the structure which seemed diminutive in comparison to Edward's story.

Alex gazed at it, so grand and so tragic. 'That's why you stay here.'

'I roamed the gardens all the time. I barely went into the house, and my father took it over, making it grand, a place that people from all over came to see.' He smiled, a broad fake smile. 'That's the story.'

'So … all the Johns are your descendants? Including Rory?'

'Yes, all of them.'

Alex wasn't sure how to ask him the obvious, but she wanted to know. 'How did you die so young, Edward?'

CHAPTER 26

Alex lay in her bed unable to sleep, her mind awhirl. She got up and looked out the window. The gazebo was dark. Edward was not there.

October 17

Dear Mum and Pa,

He died of a broken heart! After twenty years! I don't know what to think, to feel. And his brother knew! He named the manor after her, he knew! And he married the woman Edward loved. He pined for her for all that time. He would never have hurt her, he loved her.

'Nicholas loved me.' She was suddenly struck by what that meant. And Edward still loved Eleanor. He had said as much; not said, but she knew. The faraway look in his eyes, the way his eyes narrowed in pain, the stiffness of his back, the hand that clutched hers so tightly, his knuckles whitened … She would never know completely why Eleanor married his brother and he wouldn't either. But he couldn't live without her and he knew it.

But twenty years! Why did he wait that long? She was gone! Again, she thought of Nicholas. Was he waiting for her? Would he die of a broken heart? No, he had a life, things were different then. But were they? Here she was, wasting her life away, pining for things that could never be again, waiting for life to pass her by, slowly dying, waiting for … what?

Drops of rain tapped at her window and Alex walked to it in a daze. She wiped the moisture away and looked through the glass again. Still dark. She couldn't leave him alone, not with what he had just gone through telling her of his life. She threw on her slippers and her robe and walked quietly back out into the night. The air was cool, but the moon was out and pearls of water sat atop the bristles of the hedges. She walked to the centre of the gazebo and stood still.

'Edward?' She closed her eyes and felt his arm close around her waist. Droplets of water fell from her hair onto her arms and she led him out into the rain. She leaned her head on his shoulder and swayed, ignoring the goosebumps that appeared on her neck.

CHAPTER 27

There was a change in atmosphere in the house in the next week. The typical soundlessness which was usually broken by the chirp of Cathy or the curt replies to Rory by Cheryl, and sometimes, the tuneless humming of Milly, was broken by hushed arguments, a tenseness that permeated the household. When Alex walked by Cheryl, the other greeted her with a curt nod of the head, the genuine smile to which she had become accustomed was missing, and she didn't pause long enough to allow Alex to ask her how she was. Rory was the same, but at least he gave her a lopsided smile, a forced one, albeit with a frown on his face. Even Cathy was nowhere in sight and Alex missed the little girl, who sought her out to tell her about her day. And as much as Alex wanted to help, she realised they needed time to themselves, to sort out their problems without her interference.

'Things are changing already,' said Alex, walking hand in hand with Edward.

Edward nodded. 'I feel so too,' he replied and raised his chin skyward.

Alex looked up. A cloud had covered the garden. 'Looks like rain.'

'Yes,' Edward mused. 'I think that it will be time soon.'

'For what?' replied Alex, a pang hitting her chest.

He stopped walking and turned to her. 'Let's dance. It will brighten our disposition.' His eyes began to glow. Alex was not in the mood. She wanted to wallow for a while, talk to him about Cheryl and Rory ...

'Tell me about Netty,' she said suddenly. She needed to know when he would be gone, to prepare herself for his absence.

A small smile curled his lip. 'I will, but not today.' He held up her hand and twirled her around. 'Today, you will teach me.'

'Teach you what?'

'I haven't long to remain here. I want to take something of you with me.'

The pang, now a thump so loud, she was sure he heard it. 'When?' she whispered.

'Not long, Alexandra. I don't know exactly when it will

be. I'm not quite sure of how time works with me. But I will be going. I know now.'

'And you are taking Netty with you.' Her voice was small. It wasn't a question.

He didn't answer but led her back to the gazebo, his large strides making her run after him.

'No!' Alex stopped on the step and pulled her hand from him. 'You need to tell me. I need to know!' Her throat was tight and she could feel her eyes filling.

He turned to her in surprise and the line between his eyes deepened. 'You have come here to be there for the family. I see that.' He hesitated. 'And I've been brought here to lead Annette away.'

Alex shook her head to clear it. This was surreal. 'What do I have to do with anything?'

'There's a purpose for everything, Alexandra.'

'Oh, stop with the poetic bullshit!'

His eyes widened at her outburst and his lip fell slightly. 'I'm sorry.'

'Just tell me plainly what is happening.' She remained fastened to her spot on the step.

His brow knotted. 'It's what I think,' he said. 'There must be a reason for you to be here, the same as myself. I know now why I'm here. I was led to Annette; my purpose is to prepare her to leave and she must feel safe in doing so.'

'And me?'

'I don't know, but I believe you came to help.'

'Who? Rory and Cheryl?'

'Yes. And me.'

'How you? Was I supposed to keep you entertained while you waited for Netty?' She put her hands on her hip in question, a burning sensation crawling up her chest.

'Alexandra, please don't be irate with me.' He moved closer and she backed away.

'How can I not?' she demanded.

'Because I think you came here to help me, to make me love you.'

Her eyes closed and tears squeezed out. 'What about me? Why do I always lose?'

'Alexandra …'

'I have to go,' said Alex and turned on her heel and ran from him.

October 21

I knew this would happen. And I let myself believe it could last or that it wouldn't hurt me, that I would be prepared for when he left. But now I know he wasn't here for me at all. And I'm angry. I'm jealous too. I hate that he has to go and I'm just a pawn in this thing. Here for the parents, he said. Was I? Am I even helping them? Cheryl just wanders around looking lost, Rory doesn't even talk to me that much anymore. All I have is Edward and he's leaving soon, I don't even know when. And Netty. She talks about him, when he visits her, and she looks so calm and happy. Now I feel terrible; he was here for her and she needs him. I can't feel bad about that. But I do. She's going to be gone too, and soon they will all leave this place and where will I be? Back in Melbourne?

Her mind went to Nicholas again and the guilt hit her once more.

I can't go back to Nicholas. I've loved someone else … gave him my heart …

Her heart jumped. She didn't do that with Nicholas. And right now all she wanted to do was talk to Nicholas and she wished he were there to hold her, to calm her as he always did. She could never give him all of her. A jolt went through her brain. That's why she was here! She needed to love fully again, to be able to give all of her and to know that she could and it was okay to lose something or someone you love. Edward let her do that, let her know she could! She jumped up and went to the window and stared for a moment at the glow. She ran back to her writing pad, lying on the bed.

That's why I had to come here, not just for them, but for me. Love you both!

CHAPTER 28

'I won't forgive myself if she … you know … and I'm not there,' Cheryl blubbered. She couldn't even bring herself to name the inevitable. She held a tissue to her nose and Alex held a box of fresh ones.

They sat in the library where Alex had found her, Cheryl's head buried in *Gray's Anatomy,* her fingers running through lines in a page. She'd looked up guiltily when Alex entered, but moved aside on the bench to allow her to sit.

'There's nothing I can do,' she cried. 'I'm her mother. I gave her life, I should be able to save it.'

Alex peered into the book with diagrams of the human body, writings beside them. Cheryl was looking for something that didn't exist, the cure for something that was incurable. But she didn't say anything. Cheryl needed to feel like she was doing something.

'What should I do, Alex?' Cheryl closed the book and

put it on the seat beside her, still staring at it. 'I don't know what to do.'

Alex was taken aback. She was surely the last person with answers to anything, and giving any sort of advice would be remiss of her. Cheryl turned and her eyes met Alex's, who realised she was actually waiting for an answer. 'I don't know, Cheryl. Have you talked to Rory?'

Cheryl's gaze moved to the window. 'I don't know if we can make it.'

'What do you mean?'

'I can't talk to him. He wants to cheer me up, make me happy again, but I don't know how to. I can't remember the last time I was.' She turned back to Alex and her eyes were sad. 'I know it's not his fault, but when he tries to make it all better, I want to punch him.' She balled her fists tightly. 'He can't make it better and yet he carries on as if it's not happening.'

'Well, what can he do?'

'Accept that it is going to happen soon. I don't know. I don't know. She flopped her head in her hands and sobbed, her shoulders shuddering.

'What about Cathy?' Alex knew Cheryl was distraught, but it was probably time for her to face up to the fact that after Netty was gone, there were still other members of her family that needed her and that she would need too.

Cheryl looked up in surprise. 'What about her?'

'She needs you too.'

'We've had this conversation before,' Cheryl said wearily. 'And I've tried, but I can't be out having fun while ...'

'But you did have a good time ...'

'And I haven't forgiven myself yet,' she cried.

'Oh Cheryl,' said Alex, not knowing what else to say.

'There is little time left ...'

'But you may not survive it either.'

'I don't want to,' said Cheryl in a small voice and her face grew even paler in shock at what she'd just implied. 'I don't mean that.'

'Maybe you do,' replied Alex. 'Maybe you forget that there are other people who love you, who will need you. Including me.'

Cheryl looked back at her hands and every little while, a shudder went through her body.

'Netty has accepted it. She's okay with it and she's ready.'

'I'm not.'

'Okay,' said Alex, hoping that at least some of what she said had gotten through to her. She left Cheryl in the library, *Gray's Anatomy* back on her lap.

It was a Sunday afternoon and Alex wandered to the gazebo, a multitude of thoughts running through her brain. How would they survive it? What would they do? The only one at peace was Netty herself, and that was because of Edward.

Edward. She had to face him after her behaviour last night. He was just being as honest as he could, with what he knew, which really wasn't much. It wasn't his fault. She looked at the gardens to which she had poured so much love, the gardens she would have to leave soon. They looked like something out of a magazine and her mind went to Samuel, who had nodded curtly at her when he saw her after that incident. She knew he had avoided her and she was grateful for it and grateful to Edward for his interference. Yet, Samuel was going to make the family leave.

She stopped at the hedge a hundred metres from the gazebo. She didn't want to talk to Edward. He didn't understand. She turned back and quickened her step. She needed to talk to someone, to her parents. She would write them. She pulled out her notepad and began.

Dear Mum and Pa,

A tear fell on the white paper smudging the 'an', and she stopped. Nicholas's smiling face swam in her brain and she wanted to talk to him, to see his face more than anything in the world right now. She wished she wasn't so stubborn, so stupid to think she could forget him. She leaned back on her bed and pulled her phone out of her drawer. She dialled his number and hesitated, butterflies fighting in her belly. An impulse she never felt before propelled her to hit the green button and she put the phone to her ear, hearing it ring, hoping he wouldn't pick it up and wishing he would.

'Hello?' His voice low, questioning, apprehensive.

She was silent, not knowing what to say, a lump lodged in her throat.

'Blanche?'

The name she hadn't heard in so long. She fumbled and dropped the phone, quickly picking it up off the bed, and hung up, her heart thumping. He wouldn't have known it was her, he didn't have her new number, and she stared at the phone. She pushed it back in her drawer and crawled under the covers of the bed. Then she closed her eyes and for the first time, let herself think about him without hesitation.

She didn't go to the gazebo that evening, or the day after, or the day after that, avoiding working around it, and it seemed to her that Edward must have sensed her need to be alone because he didn't appear to her.

She spent the evenings in the house, talking to Cathy, who told her that Cheryl was reading to her every night.

'Mummy has been reading me Dr Seuss. Do you know that book?'

'Yes, I do,' said Alex, not telling her that Dr Seuss was the author.

'It's about a glinch,' she said and Alex smiled at the sweet innocence of this child, and a little fear ran through her heart for her. Tough times were coming and she hoped that Cheryl would continue to care for her neglected child.

And some evenings she visited with Netty, who seemed to be in a good mood lately. Alex introduced her to *Pride and Prejudice*, urging Netty to watch the serial. At first Netty had been hesitant, but with each episode, she became more involved and when Alex didn't visit for an evening, she scolded her. She had been waiting for her to keep watching it.

'He reminds me of my ghost,' said Netty of Mr Darcy, and Alex jumped. She stared at the screen and in fact could see the resemblance of Edward in the actor who played Mr Darcy. 'He comes often now. Remember when I told you the other day about how he wanted to know my favourite colour? I said red and when he came yesterday morning, he told me that he would have roses waiting with him, red ones.'

Alex swallowed. She tried not to think about Edward, but she pictured him waiting for Netty, a bunch of red roses in one hand, his gentle smile as he withdrew the arm that he held behind his back and held it to her. Like he'd done with Alex. She had to face him, and she missed him. It had been almost two weeks, but she didn't know what to say to him anymore. Her heart was sad for him, but now it wept for Nicholas, and she didn't know how to deal with what was going on all around her. And lately, she had been preparing herself. December was a month away and she had been looking at job vacancies, but nothing seemed remotely interesting or close to anything she'd found here. She'd even thought of calling Mr Sidebottom; perhaps it was time to settle down, have a place of her own, maybe even somewhere …

'Alex?' Netty was tapping lightly on her arm.

'Sorry,' said Alex, trying to work out what she had said.

'He's very cute, isn't he?'

'Yes,' replied Alex. 'Very dashing indeed.'

CHAPTER 29

It was a Saturday evening and the breeze was warm, and Alex raised her head to allow it to strain through her hair, ignoring the frizz that would inevitably pop up. It had grown so long and even with the trims Cheryl had given her, it looked unruly, crazy, everything she knew she wasn't. She sat on the bench beyond the cupid statue, hoping he would feel her there and know she wanted him to come to her. He didn't and she watched the sun set on her own, wishing he were by her side as they used to be. Now she didn't know if he would come back and the thought alarmed her. What if she never saw him again? That would mean Netty … She felt guilty knowing that Edward had been to see her 'almost every day', Netty had said, and Alex couldn't help the resentment she felt, which she knew now was irrational. She pulled herself up and walked.

'Edward,' she called as she neared the gazebo, but the muted pink of dusk mocked her. She tried again. 'I'm sorry.'

His arms came from behind, encircling her waist, and

she turned into him, burying her face in his chest. She felt his hand stroke her hair and pulled him closer, trying to regain the feeling of rest she felt in his arms.

She looked up at him. 'I want to dance with you,' she said and saw the light in his eyes. It had been nearly three weeks since she'd allowed him to whirl her around on the wooden floor of the gazebo and she missed it more than she could admit to herself.

Without a word, he raised his hand and she put hers on top of it. Wordlessly they danced, his eyes boring through hers, her own feeling the energy that poured from his. And suddenly she was on her toes, the music turning, the sounds from *Swan Lake* filling the gazebo. She let go of his hand and moved on her own, feeling the rhythm move her body the way it used to, and she closed her eyes, lost in the time of her youth. But she wasn't that youthful girl anymore, a child who had no clue about the gravity of life. She was a woman, who felt love and loss and love again, the need to care, to be cared about, to live, not wither away in the lifeless form that she'd become. She was moving fast, her arms waving, her feet barely touching the floor, her face raised to the ceiling, spinning in arabesque, gliding, darting.

Then she fell to the floor, her arms resting on her toes, and she opened her eyes. She collapsed, her face moist, her spirit spent. She knew who she was, who she was supposed to be and now, why she was here.

Edward was on one knee, his eyes shining, his lips apart, and she saw how he felt. It wasn't just Netty. She reached forward and put her lips on his cheek.

They walked through the gardens, Alex feeling like a weight had been lifted, and Edward, pride displayed on his face.

'I knew you were a dancer. All along, I knew, from the very beginning,' he said and squeezed her hand.

'It wasn't the type of dancing you taught me,' she replied, a little embarrassed that she'd let the moment sweep her away to where she almost lost consciousness—again.

'One can tell a dancer. You were born to do this.'

'Not professionally as I used to want to.' She grew silent, lost in thought, and let his hand go. She leaned on the fence and looked into the nothingness before her. A blank slate, one she wished she could be.

'Will you tell me?' asked Edward. 'What is troubling you?'

'Nothing right now.' She sighed, her spirit deflating at the amount there still was to do, the road before her. 'But everything too.'

'Can I be of any help?' He leaned on the fence beside her.

Alex turned to the garden and frowned. The camellias were starting to wilt, the heat of summer already coming before its time. She walked to them and bent down, caressing them. 'December is less than a month away. After that I don't even know …'

Edward stood silent behind her and she turned to him. He wasn't smiling, his brows knitted in thought and his head bowed.

'Then there's Netty,' she said, looking into his eyes for some reaction. There was none. She looked away into the distance. 'And then there's Nicholas.' She didn't want to see his reaction at the mention of Nicholas's name.

'Is he the man you're in love with?'

She turned to him now and saw his eyes filled with pain. 'Edward. Oh Edward. I don't know anything anymore.'

He took her hand and tucked it into his folded arms. He began to walk towards the house. 'Tell me about him.'

And she did. She told him of how much she loved Nicholas, how she couldn't just wait for the bubble to inevitably burst, she would break it herself. How she couldn't be happy, how she felt guilt at her joy and the fear that she would be left alone again.

'Just like you will do to me too,' she ended. 'That is

inevitable.'

Edward ignored her last statement. 'And you love Nicholas.'

'I thought I could forget him and when you came to me, I felt I was doing that. And then just the mention of him.' She looked at Edward. 'He came to look for me here. And I haven't stopped …'

'Then you must go to him.'

She curled into Edward's arms.

'You must go back now,' he said, smiling gently, and disappeared before her eyes. He was going to Netty. She needed him more than Alex did.

****

'Alex,' called Rory as she headed through the arch that led to the back door; she turned to see Rory heading towards the shed.

'Going out so late?'

'Just a walk tonight.'

'Is everything okay?'

'I just needed to get out for a while.'

Alex looked towards the house, which was dark, except for the light of the moon shining on the ivory stones. She wasn't keen on going back, but Edward clearly wanted her to go tonight and she wasn't in the right state of mind to be with him. 'Need some company?'

'If you want,' he said with a shrug, and Alex walked towards him.

Her own thoughts were pushed aside as she saw the pain on his face. They walked in silence towards the shed, each lost in their own thoughts, the cool breeze in the spring evening gently swaying the wildflowers that Alex couldn't bear to uproot. She hoped Samuel would find them just as beautiful as she did.

Rory stopped at the entrance, leaning on the wooden fence that led to the barn. 'I don't think I can do this much longer,' he said, his eyes shimmering.

Alex remained quiet, not knowing how to respond.

He turned to her. 'I love her so much.'

Alex wondered who he was talking about, Cheryl or Netty.

'She still can't talk to me. She is repulsed by my touch

…'

'She's going through a lot right now, Rory. Just give her some time.'

'I know I'm being selfish with everything that's going on. But I want her to lean on me. I want to be there for her. Her whole life is spent worrying about when it's going to happen.' He crushed his fist on the pole. 'And I can't do anything to help her.'

'She loves you, you know that.'

'That's just it,' he cried. 'I don't know that anymore. She's been spending more time with Cathy, and that's good, but what about me?' He sobbed into his hands now. 'I know, I'm a terrible person. How can I think about …'

'Oh Rory,' said Alex, putting her hand on his shoulder, feeling the pain he was feeling.

He was silent, his head still bowed, his shoulders bobbing, and Alex patted him. He turned to her and his face was close to hers. She suddenly saw him lean towards her and she jerked backwards.

'I'm sorry,' he cried, his astonished eyes searching her face. 'I don't know what I was doing.'

Alex was stunned, unknowing of what to do. 'Let's go back,' she said.

'I'm sorry, Alex. I don't know what came over me.'

'It's okay. I understand,' she said.

'Alex, I don't know what came over me,' he repeated. 'I'm sorry …'

'Stop saying that. I understand.' She could see the loneliness this man was feeling. She felt it herself, even when she was with other people. This was not the same as it had been with Samuel. The two brothers couldn't have been more different. This was an action born of loneliness, the need to be close to someone, anyone. And she knew how that felt. 'But I do think you should be saying these things to Cheryl, not me.'

'I know.'

****

'Was one brother not enough?' Cheryl was standing at the edge of the path, her hands on her hips, and Alex, who was pulling at weeds from the ground, shaded her eyes to look up at her.

'What do you mean?'

'I saw you! Don't deny it!'

Alex sighed and stood up. 'I don't know what ...'

'I saw it, Alex. I saw you kiss him.'

'I didn't kiss anyone,' said Alex, a little angry at the accusation. She was tired of being everyone's sounding board. And now, scapegoat.

'Then I imagined it?'

What Alex couldn't imagine was where Cheryl was when she saw it. They were a long way from the house. 'I went to find him. We had ... a fight. He was so angry.' She dropped to the stone edge now and put her head in her hands.

'Cheryl, we didn't kiss. He just needs you so much. It was just a bad reaction. He was so filled with ... I don't know, just hating himself, loving you.'

'What do I do, Alex?' Cheryl dropped down on her haunches.

'I don't know, but you have to cut him some slack, Cheryl. He doesn't know how to talk to you anymore; he thinks you hate him.'

'But I don't,' she said, looking up in astonishment. 'I just am so worried about Netty. I know it's coming, I do. But I do love him.'

'Then maybe it's time you tell him that.'

'I don't know how to,' replied Cheryl.

'Tell him how you're telling me now.'

CHAPTER 30

He didn't have to say it. She already knew. It was time. He reached for her hand and she took it, savouring the tender way his fingers clasped hers, the gentle tug as he pulled her closer. She knew it was coming and thought she might spoil it all by crying, but although she felt a lump in her chest, her tears were held at bay. She lifted her lips to his, knowing it was the last time she would feel them.

****

It was a moonless night when Netty left and Alex wandered the grounds, mourning her loss for them both, the feeling of desperation she thought she'd feel replaced by a sense of balance. She felt Netty had been happy, almost relieved that her time had come, and when Alex had seen her the night before, she'd given her a gift, her set of *Pride and Prejudice* DVDs, 'so you can see my angel,' she'd said, and her *Dirty Dancing* DVD, 'so you dance again.' Alex knew there wasn't anything she could say to help and hugged her lightly before she got up to leave.

'Alex,' said Netty, her voice small. 'Look out for my mum and dad.'

Alex nodded, not knowing what in the world she could do to help them. They would need more than her. They would need each other.

****

'She's gone,' said Rory as Alex stood in the doorway of Netty's room and she nodded. She already knew and turned to leave.

'Oh Rory,' cried Cheryl, who had been sitting beside her daughter, holding her hand.

Alex turned back to see Rory beside Cheryl, his arm around her, her head buried in his chest. They were going to be okay. As terrible as it was, this was what it would take for them to find each other again.

She walked to the kitchen, bright in comparison to the mood in the house. Milly was sitting with Cathy, a big bowl of ice cream in front of the little girl. Milly wordlessly brought out another bowl and the three of them sat in silence eating ice cream, little tears rolling down Cathy's face. Alex reached out and squeezed her hand and Cathy leapt of her stool and threw herself into Alex's arms. Alex hugged the heaving little girl, wishing she didn't have to leave. They had become family and she didn't want to think about the time when she couldn't be there for them or them for her.

CHAPTER 31

'I know this is hard,' Samuel was saying, and Alex stopped in her tracks in the hallway. She'd been on her way to the garden, which she now roamed alone in the evenings since the departure of Edward and Netty. 'But we have to work it out now.'

'The flowers on her grave are still fresh, Sam,' said Rory through gritted teeth.

Samuel cleared his throat. 'Yes, but it's what we were waiting ... I mean, there's nothing to hold you here anymore.'

Alex felt a hand on her shoulder and started. Cheryl had come up behind her and when Alex turned in surprise, she put a finger to her mouth. In the last ten days, since their daughter had passed away, Alex saw the change in them, the way she leaned on Rory, let him comfort her, how they sat huddled together with Cathy after the funeral, and when Alex walked past, motioned her over to grieve with them. They had picked a spot in the garden, close to the gazebo, in which to bury their child and Alex had filled it with red pansies, which Netty had asked for. Samuel had been silent through the whole service. He had tried to talk Rory out of burying their daughter there. 'What's the point?' he asked, but Rory dug his heels in this time and insisted she stay on the grounds. He was hoping for a miracle.

Now here was Samuel again, obviously feeling enough time had passed to broach the subject of selling the manor again.

'What do you need the money so badly for?' Rory's voice was now controlled, slow.

'That's none of your business,' Samuel returned and Alex could feel herself begin to shake. The man had no empathy, no care at all. The grip on her shoulder tightened; clearly Cheryl was also having a hard time controlling herself.

'Sam.' Rory's voice had taken a different tone. He had resorted to pleading and Alex felt her fists ball up. 'Just hang on for a little longer.'

'I have people coming in three days, Rory.' Samuel seemed to calm down a little too. 'It will depend on how long they need to settle. If they want it straight away, we have no choice.'

'You forget the house is half mine,' said Rory.

'Yes, and I also offered to pay you out.'

So it wasn't that Samuel needed the money. He would just sell it anyway, perhaps make more than he'd offer Rory. He was just a greedy man who wanted more than he had. Alex had heard enough. She shrugged Cheryl's hand off her shoulder and walked into the room. The men turned to her in surprise, Rory's face a frown, Samuel's a smirk.

'I want to make an offer,' she said, surprised at what came out of her mouth, and after his initial shock, Samuel curled up his lip in a sneer.

'Okay?' he said, crossing his arms. He was humouring her.

'I want to buy you out,' she blurted, wondering at the same time if she would have enough in her trust for it. She never wanted to know what was in there and didn't have a clue how much something like this place would cost.

Rory's eyes creased but he didn't say anything. Cheryl came up behind her, putting her hand back on her shoulder, this time trying to nudge her out of the room, but Alex shrugged it off.

'This is ridiculous,' said Samuel, turning back to Rory. 'Anyway, there are plenty of places for sale just east of the Chernut.' He ruffled some brochures on the table. 'I've looked at some and they can be moved into ...'

'What about my offer?' asked Alex, standing firm, and Samuel inhaled with irritation and looked back at her, his eyebrows raised.

'Alex,' whispered Cheryl. 'Let's take a walk.'

Alex wanted to protest but she also felt herself shaking so much she knew she should get out of the face of this man or she would explode. It wasn't often she let her emotions get the best of her in this way. 'I'm not done,' she spat at Samuel and let Cheryl walk her out.

'What was that all about?' Cheryl asked, guiding her by the elbow, out through the double doors that led to the side porch.

'I've been thinking about it,' she began. She had not been thinking anything of the sort but the moment she was faced with the situation she knew it was what she had to do. 'My mother loved her garden. It's where I got my love of it. She would have loved this place, its old-fashioned feel, the feeling of home …'

'But what's that got to do with buying it?'

'Well,' said Alex, a little uncertain now. 'I don't know how much it would be to do that, but I have a trust. Something I haven't touched since I got it. We lived in Brighton, so I assume it's quite a lot.'

'You don't know how much? You've never checked?'

'No.' She stroked the wood on the railing. 'And I've never wanted to touch it until I knew what I would want to do with it. Nothing ever seemed like it was the right thing to spend it on, you know?' She glanced at Cheryl, whose face was scrunched up in confusion. 'So I just let it stay there and honestly, I've never been one to splurge on things. It never really mattered to me. I had a good job, paid my rent ...'

'You didn't think of buying another house?'

'No, not really. I think I knew I would probably use it for that, but I don't know, it wasn't something ... I don't know how to explain it, Cheryl.'

'I get it,' replied Cheryl.

Alex's eyes brightened. 'And don't you see? It's the first time I really thought I could use it for something good. So you can keep the house ...'

'But why?'

'Oh Cheryl, you have no idea what you all have done for me.' Her eyes began to well and she turned to the gazebo, which stood a lonely structure in the light of day. All the magic it held for her had gone in the last couple of weeks. And she didn't try to get it back ... it was what she needed when she needed it. 'I'm going back to Melbourne,' she said.

Cheryl jerked backwards. 'What do you mean?'

'It's time. Have I told you about Nicholas?' She smiled now as the name rolled off her tongue. It didn't hurt anymore. And if he wasn't there anymore, then, yes, she would have to face it.

'You mentioned the name once … Wait, wasn't that the man who came here a while ago?'

'That's him.' She smiled again. 'I will tell you about him, but there's no time now.'

'But wait, if you're making an offer on the house … what will you …?'

'Just because I will be part owner doesn't mean I am going to try to take over or be a part of this family …'

'But Alex, you must know you already are!'

'Yes, I guess I do in some ways. But I also think it's time for you to be alone with yours. Become whole again, together, without intrusion.' She looked at her watch. 'I think it may be time to call the bank, see what I'm up against. Before it closes.'

'Alex, I don't know what to say. Can I dissuade you?'

'Do you want to?'

'No, I don't.'

'Then don't,' replied Alex. 'Besides, as I said, my mother would be smiling down at me right now. Even our gardens in Brighton didn't compare to this. And they were beautiful too,' she said, remembering just how beautiful.

CHAPTER 32

She followed the same winding path towards the gate and tried not to tear up when she saw them all wave to her through the rear-view mirror. The gardens looked nothing like when she had first arrived. She was glad everything had worked out, her trust only half emptied. She had ignored the pleading from Cheryl and Rory, telling her to come to her senses. Even Mr Sidebottom, who had made the trip to Chernut to work everything through with her, had asked her to give it more thought but there wasn't time, and besides, she had never been so sure of anything in her life. She just wished she could live here in the serenity of this place. She knew Nicholas would love it too—he'd always talked of moving far away from the city, having a big garden …

They disappeared from view and she thought of Nicholas and hoped he would welcome her back. If he didn't, if he had moved on, well, she would have to as well, even if she would regret it. She was in a different place now. After Edward, she knew she could give all her love to Nicholas; Edward made her see that. A feeling of guilt hit her. Even if he wasn't in the same realm as her, she had still fallen a little in love with him. And she had been able to let him go. The town of Chernut loomed ahead and Alex decided to stop at the roadside inn.

She bought her coffee and wavered, looking around at the little town. She wandered down the street and people, even though they were sparse, smiled in greeting. Amber waved at her through the window of her store, and she went down to the river to say goodbye to her swans. As she headed back to her car, she saw a picture on the glass front of a real estate agent and she was drawn to it. She read the little advertisement. It was for a cottage with a large piece of land, bushy and unkempt, not unlike Lovelet Manor when she first entered its gates. Something pinged at her heart.

Right then, she knew. It was the same ping she felt when she saw the ad for the job, the same ping when she met Edward. It was a sign, one she knew she had to follow. She pulled out her phone and took a picture of it. The she got in the car and smiled all the way back to Melbourne. She knew she would be returning.

EPILOGUE

Dear Mum and Pa,

I found it, finally.

Love you so much xx

'That's where I met Edward,' she said, her fingers intwined in Nicholas's as they stopped at the gazebo. They had just been to Netty's grave, which Alex took care of every week.

'Who's Edward?' asked Rory.

'Rory, really?' Cheryl nudged her husband in his ribs.

'Oh, Edward …' Rory still seemed uncertain. 'Yes, Edward.'

'It's okay, Rory, I know all about Edward,' said Nicholas, kissing his wife on the top of her head. 'If it wasn't for Edward, I wouldn't have got my girl back, so yeah, I guess I'm a little envious that he had more faculty than me to convince her that she loved me.' He smiled triumphantly.

'Well, no excuses,' said Rory. 'Barbeque at our place next weekend. Cathy's sixth birthday and she will not forgive you if you don't show.' He laughed. 'Besides, I'm close enough to come and find you.'

'Sorry, I know we missed the last one, but I had to go into Melbourne, hopefully for the last time. I needed to sort out the nursery.' He looked at Alex. 'Come on, we have to go. It's getting dark, and I'm worried about the wildlife on the street out here. I nearly hit a wombat the other day.'

They turned to go but Alex hesitated. 'Can you give me a minute?'

'Sure,' said Nicholas. 'But if he tries to steal you away, I'm prepared for a fight, no matter what realm it's in.' The three of them left her alone.

She stood quietly in front of the gazebo, Alex remembering her first dance with Edward with fondness. If it weren't for him, she would never have gone back to dancing. Not competitively as she once hoped for, but dancing with Nicholas, as uncoordinated as he first seemed, was enough for her. Their house was filled with music now and she hoped it would pass on to the little thing growing inside her. She rubbed her tummy absently and looked to the skies. She thought about them without resentment now, allowed herself to enjoy who they were to her, and even though she still missed them, she knew they were there with her.

She knew someone else was too.

'Thank you, Edward,' she whispered, and a sliver of sun broke through the clouds.

The End

Thank you for reading this book and I do hope you enjoyed it.

If you did, please take a few moments to leave a review.

This can be done on:

Amazon: https://www.amazon.com.au/Rita-H-Rowe/e/B085WNQCHG/ref=dp_byline_cont_pop_ebooks_1

Goodreads: https://www.goodreads.com/author/show/20152771.Rita_H_Rowe

Website: https://www.ritahrowe.com/

Or feel free to add a review or a rating anywhere you like.

Thank you again.

Rita H Rowe

ABOUT THE AUTHOR

Rita H Rowe has a passion for words, encouraged by a mother who spent most of her spare time with her head buried in a book. Of course she was going to become dazzled by the words of Enid Blyton, Louisa May Alcott and later on, the likes of Sidney Sheldon and even the early works of Harold Robbins. Her tastes are diverse, and she can go straight from Margaret Mitchell and Alexandre Dumas to Liane Moriarty and Jeffrey Archer in the blink of an eye.

It was finding her own style that was problematic. Trying to create stories in the same vein as her gurus was not fulfilling and in 2019, she embarked on a Masters in Writing. She discovered her passion and established her style; so keen was she to get going, that by the end of the year, she had published her first novel, Never The Moon.

Most of Rowe's work deals with the human condition, particularly from a woman's point of view, which at times draws on her own experiences and that of others, with their permission of course.

Rowe lives with her family and teaches secondary school English and Art in Melbourne.

Find out more about Rita H Rowe

Website: https://www.ritahrowe.com/

Facebook: https://www.facebook.com/ritahrowe/

Instagram: https://www.instagram.com/ritahrowe_writes/

Other Novels by Rita H Rowe

Never The Moon

Two men who couldn't be more different. One woman caught between them.

Jennifer lost the love of her life. David married another woman, and that was it. Over. Finished.

Fleeing to New York for a fresh start and a new chance at life, Jennifer meets Jack—rugged and handsome. He's everything she thought she could never have.

But things are never as easy as they should be and Jennifer's whole world is plunged into chaos and violence once more. An abusive husband, a loveless marriage—and no way out.

When David comes barrelling back into Jennifer's life, she's torn between the men once again, but the stakes couldn't be higher.

Never the Moon interweaves the lives of Jennifer, David and Jack, revealing the power of love and the destruction it can leave in its wake.

She Remembered

Her beauty is a curse. Her memories a void.

Elena cannot remember. All she has are fragments of a past life that feel foreign to her, only glimpsed in fleeting moments through violent nightmares.

Struggling to put her life together and find acceptance, she takes comfort in Luke, a charming boy who seems to like her as much as she likes him. But nothing has ever come easily to Elena—and when she wakes up between blood-soaked sheets next to the body of a man recently stabbed, what little stability she had comes crashing down around her.

With no one to help her and nowhere to go, Elena has to salvage the broken pieces of her life all on her own. If only she could remember …

The Bad Seed

Love, betrayal and murder.

He's the new kid in town, complete with a sordid past and a tarnished family name, doomed to fail even before he begins. Jenna is the only person who sees beyond Joey's past and they fall deeply in love.

But there are already forces determined to separate the pair by any means necessary. Tommy, the thug, who is hell-bent on breaking Joey by brute force, Jenna's mother, whose connection with Joey cannot be ignored, and Joey's own past, the strongest weapon against them.

Only Tim, the local police officer, shows any compassion to the plight of Joey and Jenna, but is Tim all he seems? And what role will he play in their fate?

Can young love survive in a town filled with discrimination? Can Joey and Jenna get out before they fall apart, or is it already too late?

Becoming Ruthless

When all the men she knows are liars, maybe it's time to become one too.

Ruth is young, excited about life and not looking for love. Yet love finds her, and Ruth is thrilled. But she is left devastated when she finds out that her the man she loves has deceived her. Still hopeful, she embarks on another relationship only to find herself in the same predicament.

Ruth becomes disenchanted with love and decides that if she can't beat them, she may as well join them and begins a journey that will change her very being and endanger her life.

Can Ruth find herself before it's too late? Or will she become what she has always despised—a loathsome liar?